Sword Art: Or

Gun Ga

5th Squad Jam: Start

Keiichi Sigsawa

ILLUSTRATION BY

Kouhaku Kuroboshi

SUPERVISED BY

Reki Kawahara

CONTENTS

Chapter 1: Fifth Time's the Charm
001

Chapter 2: Bounty, Thy Name Is Llenn
039

Chapter 3: Alone in the Mist
063

Chapter 4: A Battle for Two
095

Chapter 5: Converging
133

Sword Art Online Alternative
GUN GALE ONLINE
XI
5th Squad Jam: Start

DESIGN: BEE-PEE

Sword Art Online Alternative
GUN GALE ONLINE XI
5th Squad Jam: Start

Sword Art Online Alternative

GUN GALE ONLINE XI

5th Squad Jam: Start

Keiichi Sigsawa

ILLUSTRATION BY
Kouhaku Kuroboshi

SUPERVISED BY
Reki Kawahara

NEW YORK

SWORD ART ONLINE Alternative Gun Gale Online Vol. 11
KEIICHI SIGSAWA

Translation by Stephen Paul
Cover art by Kouhaku Kuroboshi

This book is a work of fiction. Names, characters, places, and incidents are the product of the author's imagination or are used fictitiously. Any resemblance to actual events, locales, or persons, living or dead, is coincidental.

First published in Japan in 2021 by KADOKAWA CORPORATION, Tokyo.
English translation rights arranged with KADOKAWA CORPORATION, Tokyo, through TUTTLE-MORI AGENCY, INC., Tokyo.

Yen On
150 West 30th Street, 19th Floor
New York, NY 10001

Visit us at yenpress.com * facebook.com/yenpress * twitter.com/yenpress *
yenpress.tumblr.com * instagram.com/yenpress

First Yen On Edition: November 2022
Edited by Yen On Editorial: Payton Campbell
Designed by Yen Press Design: Andy Swist

Yen On is an imprint of Yen Press, LLC.
The Yen On name and logo are trademarks of Yen Press, LLC.

The publisher is not responsible for websites (or their content) that are not owned by the publisher.

Library of Congress Cataloging-in-Publication Data
Names: Sigsawa, Keiichi, 1972– author. | Kuroboshi, Kouhaku, illustrator. |
Kawahara, Reki, supervisor. | Paul, Stephen (Translator), translator.
Title: Fifth Squad Jam: Start / Keiichi Sigsawa ; illustration by Kouhaku Kuroboshi ; supervised by Reki Kawahara ; translation by Stephen Paul ; cover art by Kouhaku Kuroboshi.
Description: First Yen On edition. | New York : Yen On, 2018– |
Series: Sword art online alternative gun gale online ; Volume 11
Identifiers: LCCN 2018009303 | ISBN 9781975327521 (v. 1 : pbk.) |
ISBN 9781975353841 (v. 2 : pbk.) | ISBN 9781975353858 (v. 3 : pbk.) |
ISBN 9781975353865 (v. 4 : pbk.) | ISBN 9781975353872 (v. 5 : pbk.) |
ISBN 9781975353889 (v. 6 : pbk.) | ISBN 9781975315320 (v. 7 : pbk.) |
ISBN 9781975315979 (v. 8 : pbk.) | ISBN 9781975315993 (v. 9 : pbk.) |
ISBN 9781975321802 (v. 10 : pbk.) | ISBN 9781975348564 (v. 11 : pbk.)
Subjects: | CYAC: Fantasy games—Fiction. | Virtual reality—Fiction. Y Role playing—Fiction. |
BISAC: FICTION / Science Fiction / Adventure.
Classification: LCC PZ7.1.S537 Sq 2018 | DDC [Fic]—dc23
LC record available at https://lccn.loc.gov/2018009303

ISBNs: 978-1-9753-4856-4 (paperback)
978-1-9753-4857-1 (ebook)

10 9 8 7 6 5 4 3 2 1

LSC-C

Printed in the United States of America

CHAPTER 1
Fifth Time's the Charm

SECT.1

CHAPTER 1
Fifth Time's the Charm

September 12th, 2026.

Just seven minutes before twenty hundred hours, meaning eight o'clock on this Saturday evening, Llenn heard Pitohui give her a greeting that was so abbreviated, she couldn't tell what was being said: "Geev!"

In fact, it might not have been a greeting at all. Pitohui may have simply decided to make a silly sound with her mouth upon seeing Llenn.

They were, of course, inside *Gun Gale Online*, the full-dive VR game that employed all the bodily senses. They were located in the entirely digital city of SBC Glocken, in a private room contained within what looked like a western saloon.

Llenn, whose diminutive avatar was no more than five feet tall and clad in her usual faded-pink combat fatigues—albeit under the dark-brown robe she wore in town to hide her identity—had just entered the room in the saloon.

"Good evening, Pito. Is it just you?"

The room featured a round table large enough to seat ten people, but there was only one person present: a slender woman wearing a navy-blue bodysuit, her black hair tied high in a ponytail, and with geometric-patterned tattoos on her cheeks.

In short, she was the quintessential Pitohui.

But in as deep a voice as she could manage, she muttered, "The truth is, it's me, M… I woke up this morning, and we had switched bodies…"

"Iced tea," Llenn said in response to this shocking admission.

A cup with a straw and a lid popped up out of the surface of the table. Llenn doffed her robe—by swiping with her hand on her menu, not by physically taking off the item—and sat down.

"C'mon, Llenn, you're no fun!" Pitohui pouted. But the truth was that if you were going to react to something like that, you'd never last on Pitohui's team.

Llenn scooted her chair up to the table, lifted her cup of iced tea with tiny hands, and asked, "Shall we make a toast, Pito?"

"Oh, fine, if you insist. Cheers!"

Pitohui lifted a large mug from the table. The contents, green and brown, as if the drink were made of liquefied locusts, were a mystery.

After giving their cup and mug a little kiss, the two of them downed their beverages. Once their virtual throats were virtually refreshed, Pitohui launched into a grave, dignified speech.

"I believe you all know the reason I have gathered you here tonight…"

"No one else is here!"

"Ah. Thank you for that interruption."

Llenn failed to keep ignoring her nonsense.

About ten minutes later, Pitohui repeated, "I believe you all know the reason I have gathered you here tonight…"

This time, there were others gathered around the table.

Next to Llenn sat Fukaziroh. She had her blond hair tied up in her usual style and was wearing a MultiCam shirt and shorts, plus tights.

Across the table was Shirley. She wore a forest camo jacket with very realistic tree-bark patterns on it. Because they were indoors, she wasn't wearing a hat, leaving her brilliant short green hair visible.

On the other side of Shirley was Clarence. She wore all-black combat gear that looked like it belonged to a special police unit, and her face was masculine and handsome, like a Takarazuka actor who specialized in male roles.

And then there was M, a man built like a bear, wearing a green T-shirt. As usual, for bottoms he wore his green camo combat pants.

It was the lineup of six who fought together in SJ4, as well as the recent Five Ordeals quest. Yes, you might even call them teammates.

"It's so we can talk about what we're doin' with the fifth Squad Jam, right? They sent out the registration message earlier today confirming the event," Clarence replied.

Honk-honk. A whimsical sound filled the room.

It was Pitohui, holding a horn with a rubber sphere on one end, and squeezing it to produce the noise. When did she get that out?

It was a rubber honking horn, more properly known as a bulb horn. In real life, you could buy one at a big musical instrument store or on the Internet.

This was the first time that Llenn knew it was in *GGO*, too. But she didn't know *why*. Nor did she know why Pitohui had one. It was probably pointless to wonder.

"Correct!" Pitohui exclaimed.

"Yesss!" cheered Clarence.

"Why would we come here if not for that?" Shirley grumbled sourly. In short, the way she always did.

But she was likely concerned that the conversation was never going to move forward if she didn't prod it along, so she continued, "We're gonna go with this group for SJ5 again, right? I get it. I'm in. We'll be seeded, so we don't need to bother with the qualifying round. I'll make sure I'm there on time the day of the event. The end. Can I go now?"

With that, she put her lips on the straw of her iced coffee, no cream, with syrup. She was determined to finish the entire thing before she left the room.

"Now, now, Shirl, don't jump to conclusions," Pitohui said, waving the horn.

"Don't call me that."

"Fine, fine. Anyway, listen closely, everyone—including Shirley. Today we're going to be talking about the special rules, all right?"

Fukaziroh stopped sipping her lemon soda to ask, "What's all this about special rules? They got some newfangled restrictions on us?"

Did you not read the damn message? thought Llenn.

At least she knew this Fukaziroh was indeed the real Fukaziroh. She'd have been a different person entirely if she had actually read the message beforehand.

"You didn't really read the message again, did you, Fuka?"

Honk-honk.

What is the point of that horn? Llenn wondered but did not say aloud.

Pitohui waved her left hand and operated a floating window that only she could see. The only thing visible was the way her fingers moved and tapped the air.

A large screen appeared on the far wall of the room. The wall had been covered in floral wallpaper, but it instantly turned into a screen measuring over a hundred inches, displaying a message.

This was an area where the virtual world was incredibly convenient. If you got used to it, the real world seemed so clumsy in comparison.

"Here's the message that went out about SJ5 earlier today. Let's do a little refresher. Fuka, you'll be in charge of scrolling the text."

1:00 PM, September 12th, 2026.

To my dear friends.

How are you? I am doing well.

This message is being sent to all players who have appeared in any Squad Jam (henceforth "SJ") event.

As I probably don't even need to point out, I am the novelist sponsor, the one who came up with the idea for SJ.

Thank you to everyone who took part in my recent simultaneous competitive quest, Five Ordeals.

But you had all kinds of nasty things to say about me online, didn't you?

Like, "What kind of horrible ending is this?"

Or, "Screw you, jerk!"

And, "I'm a cat person anyway!"

All right, maybe the last one isn't actually an insult. Just for the record, I don't mind cats. I'm just allergic to them.

Anyway, it made me quite sad to read such horrible reactions to my very earnest event.

But this message isn't about revenge. I'll choose to ignore my pain.

I don't bear a grudge over it. No, I'm not seething with enmity in the least... I'm not seeking retribution at all...

* * *

"Oh wow, he's really upset about this. I guess he's the kind of guy who can't get over things easily," Fukaziroh noted immediately, pausing the message.

No one disagreed with this observation; they just nodded in silence. Everyone taking part in Squad Jam understood by now that the sponsor was a waste of life who was much too old to be so immature. It was old news.

"I wonder if he was able to take our glorious fight against the mecha-dragon and use it to write his novel," Pitohui said. Nobody could give her an answer, because nobody cared.

Fukaziroh ran her finger along the window to scroll the text on the giant screen, moving on to the next part.

As for what I want to say with this message, I can sum it up in a single sentence.

We're doing a fifth SJ! Right away!

Okay, that was two sentences.

@SJ5 basic info.
Time: September 19th, 2026 (Sat.), 1:00 PM (Japan Time) start
Eligible teams: 30 in total (max 6 members per team)

You're able to register as of this very moment! Click right here to sign up! The deadline is midnight on September 17th!

Just as always, any team that has placed within the top four of any SJ event will be seeded, so you will be automatically granted entry.

However, you may not split up your members and enter as multiple teams.

All other teams, if the total entries exceed the number of slots for the event, will participate in a preliminary competition on the day before the event, September 18th, starting at seven PM, so be sure you're available.

The qualifying round will play out the same way it always does: head-to-head fights on long, straight maps.

As most of you probably know, you don't need to have your entire team present to take part in the qualifying round. If you think you can destroy your opponents alone, try it out!

Fukaziroh paused here and noted, "The nineteenth is really soon. It hasn't even been a month since the last one. What's he in such a rush for? Am I not gonna have time to go back to *ALO* again?"

Her primary VR game was *ALfheim Online*, generally known as *ALO*. It was a beautiful fantasy world where players inhabited different kinds of winged fairies, flying through the sky and going on adventures in picturesque surroundings.

It was quite different from *GGO*, where mankind came back to a future Earth devastated by a civilization-ending war and were reduced to crawling around the ruins of their giant spaceship, killing one another for loot. Completely different, in fact.

When SJ2 happened, Fukaziroh decided to help Llenn out by converting: moving her character from one game to the other, a process that maintained the character's relative strength. She'd done it several times by now.

And she'd stayed in *GGO* ever since SJ4, including the recent quest.

"You still haven't gone back…? No wonder you showed up so fast," Llenn marveled.

The main point, however, was that Fukaziroh in *GGO* was a very powerful presence, so all was well! In fact, she could stay permanently in *GGO*, if she wanted to help…?

Pitohui said, "Just so we're all on the same page, I trust that nobody has any big errands to run on that date at that time? We're all good?"

She glared at everyone except for M. It was a glare that did not allow for any refusal. A glare that said, *If you have any small errands, too bad; you're still coming along.*

"Nothing aside from studying for my college tests," Llenn replied.

"Watch out, Llenn. You're giving away your identity. Remember, aren't you supposed to be a housewife with three nursing children to take care of?" Fukaziroh remarked.

"So they're triplets? Are they cute?" wondered Clarence.

"Were you actually paying attention to anything anyone said?" Shirley asked, worried about her partner's intelligence. "Anyway, I'm fine. If I couldn't have made it to SJ5, I wouldn't be showing up for this meeting."

"Okay, so we're all in," Pitohui concluded, satisfied. She did not honk the horn this time.

Oh, Pito's already bored of the horn, Llenn thought but did not say aloud.

"As for the most important people of all, me and M, we're perfectly open, of course! I had a really important piece of work that day, but I just axed it right off the calendar."

Don't do that! Come on! You're Elza Kanzaki! Llenn thought furiously but did not say aloud. She could never say that aloud.

"Wow. So despite the way you look, you have a job and stuff? What do you do, Pito?" Clarence asked cluelessly.

"I'm not interested. Keep talking about Squad Jam," Shirley urged.

That's right—these two have no idea that Pito is Elza Kanzaki. I wonder how they'd react if they found out, Llenn thought but of course did not say aloud. She could never.

"Go ahead, then, Fuka. Let's continue. The special rules this time are extra complicated," Pitohui urged.

* * *

@About SJ5's special rules.

The basic rules are the same as previous Squad Jams.

A Satellite Scan will reveal the location of the team leaders and team names every ten minutes, and leadership passes down in succession if the leader gets killed—you can read the attached rule book for all the usual details. But the real draw of Squad Jam is the "special rules," which change every time!

Yes! We're doing it again!

Now, about the special rules…

There are two broad categories: those that can be explained beforehand (i.e., now) and those that will only be revealed once the Squad Jam battle is under way.

The latter will be displayed within the game as they become active. Have fun! Enjoy being startled!

So here, I'll only explain the special rules that can be revealed at this time.

Read them carefully and only take part in the event if you agree to them. (Meaning: Don't whine about it afterward.)

I've got an all-new, groundbreaking idea…

"Switching your entire loadout with the help of your teammate (henceforth 'gear-switching') is now possible."

I'll list the rules regarding alternate gear below. Read them carefully so that you understand them.

Rule 1

"All SJ5 players in the final event will be able to carry a set of alternate gear for one of your teammates, with no effect on your weight limit, within your item storage."

Rule 2

"Alternate gear contains everything, including weapon ammunition and other eligible items usable within Squad Jam. The upper limit is the amount by weight that the owning player can carry."

Rule 3

"Alternate gear is exchanged via a gear-switch with your currently equipped loadout. You cannot use both sets at the same time. Gear you don't want to trade (your regular clothing, defensive items, etc.) can be retained in your inventory."

Rule 4

"Gear-switching is only possible when the carrying teammate is close by, within the range for ordinary item exchanges."

Rule 5

"If the teammate dies, the alternate gear they are carrying is no longer usable within the battle in any way."

Rule 6

"You cannot materialize and use the set of alternate gear you are carrying for your teammate."

Rule 7

"Gear that your teammate has received and materialized can be loaned to you for use. If the teammate dies in battle, it will continue to be usable, as will enemy gear, which can be plundered in the same way as before."

Rule 8

"If your teammate uses the gear-switch function while you are using their alternate gear, it will disappear and no longer be in your possession."

Rule 9

"The alternate gear set can be registered in an item list that does not interfere with carrying capacity before you enter the

waiting area at the bar. During the ten minutes in the waiting area before the battle, you may choose which set you will use."

Rule 10

"You are free to choose who in your team will carry whose gear prior to the start of the battle. During the battle, you cannot alter who carries the gear."

Rule 11

"Alternate gear is optional. You may take part in the battle without making use of it."

The end.

"Mm-hmm. I see. An entire set of alternate gear that you can switch between... Quite a special set of rules, indeed... Why, I'd say I've never seen such a system before...in my sixty-five years of VR gaming..."

"Thank you, mysterious old man. Also, no VR game is that old," Llenn said, telling Fukaziroh off. It would be cruel to simply ignore her comment. Humoring her is just what a friend would do.

"Now, I believe you all know the reason I have gathered you here tonight," said Pitohui for the third time this evening. "We need to figure this one out. We'll want to increase the variety of gear—mostly weaponry—and I want to work on our overall team balance. It'll change the way we fight, too."

While her tone of voice was fairly brief and flippant, Pitohui's topic was a smart and diligent one. She could be normal if she wanted to be.

Clarence raised her hand and called out, "Sensei, hang on. I didn't actually understand all of the rules. Did everyone else follow the whole thing perfectly? Did you guys all get perfect grades in school?"

"Good point. Shall we refresh the entire list from the top?" suggested Miss Pitohui.

"Yes, Sensei!" said Clarence the student. It was good to be obedient and an attentive listener.

Llenn understood the rules after reading them several times, but maybe she just *thought* she understood. It never hurt to go back over them.

Pitohui waved her left arm and produced an automatic pistol from her inventory. It was a simple-looking weapon like a series of boxes stuck together: the Glock 34. Pitohui did not normally use this gun.

On the underside of the gun was a device like a combination laser sight and flashlight. Pitohui turned on the green laser and held the Glock in her right hand, pointing it at the wall.

In other words, she only took out the gun to use it as a laser pointer. This was the sort of thing that good little gun-loving children should never do in the real world, whether with a real gun or a model. It would be a bad, bad idea.

Pitohui pointed the green light at the first rule, underlining the words as she read them off.

"All SJ5 players in the final event will be able to carry a set of alternate gear for one of your teammates, with no effect on your weight limit, within your item storage.

"This one is...well, pretty self-explanatory. Any questions, Clare?"

"I get this part. You won't get weighed down by someone else's gear. That's a good thing."

Llenn considered this one, too. It was a natural system—if carrying someone else's gear meant you couldn't carry your own, it would be no different from the way things worked regularly.

The main point of this special rule set was that you could carry someone else's gear without it weighing anything. It meant that Llenn, who had the smallest carrying capacity on the team, could haul the gear for M, the heaviest.

"Okay, let's look at rule two."

"Alternate gear contains everything, including weapon ammunition and other eligible items usable within Squad Jam. The upper limit is the amount by weight that the owning player can carry."

Pitohui followed the sentences with the green dot.

"Any problem?"

"Actually, I wanted to ask about this one and number three together."

"Okay, okay."

"Alternate gear is exchanged via a gear-switch with your currently equipped loadout. You cannot use both sets at the same time. Gear you don't want to trade (your regular clothing, defensive items, etc.) can be retained in your inventory."

Clarence said, "This was the part I had trouble with. What does it mean?"

It was indeed tricky, Llenn thought.

Miss Pitohui explained, "To put it simply, it means you don't have to exchange *everything*. So you don't need to also switch your clothing. Do you even have another outfit, Clare?"

"Nope! Only this one! Black highlights a woman's beauty!" Clarence said proudly.

"Ahhh, the wisdom of Coco Chanel. You're pretty wise for someone who looks so dumb," said Fukaziroh.

"Huh? No, it's a quote from *Kiki's Delivery Service*," Clarence replied.

"Oh, that one. Well, I went and smothered you in kindness you didn't deserve," Fukaziroh grumbled.

Miss Pitohui ignored them both. "In that case, your clothing and boots and such don't need to be exchanged, so they will always count toward your weight limit, see? If they make up five percent of your carrying capacity, for example, then the other ninety-five percent is for your weapons and stuff, which means your alternate gear has to be the same ninety-five percent weight or lower."

"Ohhh, I get it. So you can't just bring way more in your alternate set that you wouldn't be able to carry anyway, and switch it out when you want to use it," Clarence said, quick on the uptake.

Llenn, too, had been hoping she might be able to fit more ammo than she could actually carry in her alternate gear set. That wouldn't be happening, it turned out.

"Okay, on to the next one..."

The green dot traced the fourth rule.

"Gear-switching is only possible when the carrying teammate is close by, within the range for ordinary item exchanges."

"Oh, I get that one! It's just like normal items!" Clarence said, so they moved on to rule five.

"If the teammate dies, the alternate gear they are carrying is no longer usable within the battle in any way."

"Since it says 'within the battle,' that means that once SJ5 is over, everything will come safely back to you, right?" Clarence asked skeptically.

Pitohui reassured her that this was the case.

"Whew! That's good to hear," Clarence said, and Llenn echoed her feelings. If her teammate dying meant P-chan died, too, that would be tragic. She'd lost her P90 twice already in Squad Jams, and she didn't want it to happen a third time.

"Next, then..."

Pitohui waved the Glock 34 and thus the green laser attached to it.

"You cannot materialize and use the set of alternate gear you are carrying for your teammate."

"I get that one, too! Of course you can't just use all their stuff."

"Okay, number seven."

"Gear that your teammate has received and materialized can be loaned to you for use. If the teammate dies in battle, it will continue to be usable, as will enemy gear, which can be plundered in the same way as before."

"About this one," Clarence said with a grin. But in truth, she was always grinning, so it was really *even more* of a grin. "Does that mean that if I'm dying, I can switch to the set of gear that has more ammo and materialize all of it really quickly so that my teammates can pick it up right after I die?"

"Oh, you have some wicked ideas," Pitohui replied.

Ahhh, so you could potentially do that, huh? Llenn realized. She hadn't thought about it when reading the rules. Apparently, she just wasn't wicked enough.

"If your teammate uses the gear-switch function while you are using their alternate gear, it will disappear and no longer be in your possession."

As for rule eight, Clarence remarked, "That makes sense! It wouldn't be fair, otherwise."

On to number nine.

"The alternate gear set can be registered in an item list that does not interfere with carrying capacity before you enter the waiting area at the bar. During the ten minutes in the waiting area before the battle, you may choose which set you will use."

"About this one, ten minutes is a pretty short time to pick out your stuff, right? Shouldn't we have it all set up before going in?" Clarence asked.

M replied, "Absolutely. Especially if you can pack right up to your carrying limit."

Llenn thought, *I want to bring every single magazine my weight capacity allows. So I'll need to do a bit of preparation.*

"Okay, got it. That's all I wanted to ask."

"Next up, rule ten."

Pitohui waved the green dot.

"You are free to choose who in your team will carry whose gear prior to the start of the battle. During the battle, you cannot alter who carries the gear."

"So if I'm understanding things correctly, this means anyone can carry anyone else's gear?"

"Yep."

"But if you think about it...normally, it makes the most sense if you and your partner carry each other's stuff, right?"

"Indeed. Normally, you would do that. If you need a reason that isn't normal, then you wouldn't."

"What reason would that be?" Clarence asked.

Pitohui shrugged with dramatic abandon. It was the kind of shrug that actual Japanese people never did.

Apparently, she couldn't think of a reason. Or she could, but it was a secret she wanted to keep from her own teammates.

"Hmph. Well, whatever. Lastly, the eleventh rule...

"Alternate gear is optional. You may take part in the battle without making use of it."

"Yep, got it! No problems here! I dunno, I feel it would be a waste not to make use of the special rules, you know? Who isn't gonna use them?"

"Me. Right here. I only use my sniper rifle. No other guns. No need for alternate gear," said Shirley, breaking her silence resolutely.

She was indeed intensely specced out for sniping, so that made sense. All she needed was her favorite bolt-action rifle, the Blaser R93 Tactical 2, and her homemade insta-kill exploding bullets.

"What?! But what about the rifle pistol you used in SJ4?" Clarence asked.

Clarence had blown up spectacularly before the gun made its appearance, but she knew that Shirley made her mark inside the mall, where only pistols were allowed, by using the Remington XP-100, a handgun like a shortened rifle. That was because it was Clarence who chose the gun, at Shirley's request.

"I'm not using that one. There's no point unless it's in a pistols-only area."

"Bummer!"

"I've kept it around, though, as a commemoration."

"Awww, that's so nice!"

Pitohui remarked, "Yes, I suppose that's best for Shirley. And it says later on that there will be ammo refills this time, too. So go ahead and blast away with those explosive rounds."

No one was inclined to argue, so it was decided that Shirley was fine with just the one set of gear.

"In that case, I no longer have any need to be here," she said impatiently. "I'm going to get some shooting practice in."

"You *do* need to be here!" said Clarence. "We need to figure out who in the team has what! And we need to figure out who's carrying whose gear! It's really important!"

In times like these, you could count on Clarence to be smart. She was quite the gamer.

"……"

Shirley paused in the act of standing up and, without having a good answer, ultimately sat back down and ordered another iced coffee, no cream, with simple syrup. It appeared from out of the table at once.

"Let's start by figuring out everyone's second loadout. We can decide whose gear Shirley will carry after that," declared Pitohui, returning the Glock 34 to her inventory. Apparently, they were going to go with the term *second loadout* for the alternate set of gear the teammate would carry.

"Excuse me, Pito," said Llenn, raising her pink arm. She was raising her hand, but it was her arm that was pink.

"Go ahead, Llenn!"

Honk-honk.

Pitohui hadn't forgotten about the horn on the table after all.

"I'm not going to be using any gun aside from P-chan for my main weapon, either. But I might carry around Vor-chan as a sub-weapon."

Her teammates didn't need to ask, because they already knew, but she called her main P90 by the name of "P-chan," and the set of two Vorpal Bunny pistols together were "Vor-chan." All of her weapons were colored pink.

"Awww, why not take the opportunity to use a different one? C'mon, it'll be way more très fun!" Fukaziroh pouted. Her attempt at French was not exactly correct, but the point was made.

"Ugh. I don't want to have to learn how to use a whole new gun at this point. And even if it works out, I'm not going to be better at it than with the guns I already have," Llenn admitted.

Fukaziroh's brow wrinkled. "Alas...kids these days... No patience, no commitment..."

"Oh, are you still Grandpa?"

"Ahhh, my cute little Llenn... Listen to the advice your grandpa has for you."

"Hee-hee-hee. Am I really cute?"

"It's more like a nickname. Don't take it seriously."

"Sheesh!"

"Listen... Being able to switch your loadout means...you have the ability to take your opponent by surprise. Have you forgotten about the ending of the Five Ordeals the other day...the sixth ordeal?"

"Hrm… Yeah, I guess so."

She had a point.

Llenn had completed the *sixth* ordeal, a totally unnecessary event at the end of the quest. It was the part that devolved into a battle with the rest of the team over whether or not to kill the dog.

In that battle, Llenn and Fukaziroh switched their outfits. Fukaziroh used the P90 and blasted away, taking Pitohui and Boss by surprise. She didn't land a single shot, but it *had* taken them by surprise.

"That's right," said M, his voice a rumble among the others. "That's the biggest benefit of the second loadout: You can surprise the enemy. There are videos of all Squad Jams, and we've been through several. Everyone's watched and studied one another, and knows the other players' weapons and tactical style. We're fighting naked out there."

"It's too bad we can't actually be naked. I wanna feel the breeze against my nips."

"Shut up, Clarence," Shirley snapped.

M pretended he didn't hear them. "Naturally, the participants are going to hone their strategies for one another. But an alternate gear set allows you to counteract that. I think we should make full use of this system. The other teams are undoubtedly going to use every trick in the book. Shirley's sniping with explosive rounds and no bullet line is the exception—the other five of us should decide on a second weapon and, as much as time allows, practice with it. We can't hope to win this one without making that effort."

"A very good point from M! He stole all the bits I wanted to say! Thanks for nothing, jerk!"

Honk-honk.

"Well, in that case…" Llenn had no choice but to accept. If you were going to appear in Squad Jam, you had to aim for the best possible result. That was the point, and anything less would be rude to the rivals they'd fought along the way.

Plus, she just wanted to win. Oooh, she wanted to win. Man, she sure wanted to win.

"Oh, but before that, keep reading, Fuka. The part about ammo replenishing," Pitohui urged.

"Mm-hmm," Fukaziroh murmured, scrolling downward.

@About the replenishment of ammunition and energy in SJ5.

This is another special rule for this event, so pay attention.

And by the way, you'll be able to consult this rule book at any time during Squad Jam, too.

For the first hour, there will be two (full) recovery periods, at thirty minutes and the hour.

There will be no automated recovery points after that.

However: You will recover when defeating another player.

If you finish off (land the last attack) on a player, you will recover every one of your equipped guns' ammunition or energy up to a certain amount, depending on the current percentage remaining of your total.

0–10% remaining: recover up to 50%.

11–30% remaining: recover up to 60%.

31–50% remaining: recover up to 70%.

51–79% remaining: recover up to 80%.

If you have over 80% of your ammo/energy left, you will not recover any.

An extra note.

The remaining ammo/energy percentage can be displayed by

going to the "remaining shots display" setting in the options and turning on "show percentage." I would recommend making that visible during SJ5.

Of course, only the weapons in the set you're holding and using will recover. You won't get any ammo back for the set your teammate is carrying for you.

Also, if the system determines that multiple people defeated the same target (extremely unlikely), every one of them will recover all their ammo.

"See, you spawn in, and you can fire away without holding back at all. Once you get into the mid stages and beyond, you gotta make sure you're killin' folks; otherwise, those wasted shots will start to add up. Guess it's a special rule meant to prevent the strategy that won SJ2, running and hiding."

Fukaziroh picked up on the idea behind the ammo replenishment quite quickly. That just went to show how good of a gamer Fukaziroh was. Llenn had to read the memo a few times to understand how it worked.

"'See, you spawn in'?" Fukaziroh continued, "More like *Gee-oh-vawn-i.* Giovanni and Campanella...you know what I mean?"

Llenn did not know what she meant. Something about the sound of the first phrase made Fukaziroh think of the name Giovanni and made her want to say something pretentious.

That was good old airheaded Fukaziroh for you. Llenn had been friends with her for years, and she still didn't get Fuka.

"Whoa! Are you a fan of *Night on the Galactic Railroad,* Fuka?" asked Clarence, latching on. The topic was threatening to get truly derailed.

"All right, I'm cutting you off there," said Miss Pitohui before the class started talking about the classic writer Kenji Miyazawa.

Llenn said, "Well, that gives me an idea, actually… Since we got a ton of money from the last quest, I could probably buy just about any weapon I want… So what is everyone aside from Shirley going to use for their backup?"

She wasn't asking them to tell her what to do. She was just being proactive about taking everything else into account when making her choice, she thought.

"Good question," Pitohui replied. "It's a tough choice for me, since, as you know, I'm good with just about anything, but I'm thinking of taking in a 7.62 mm machine gun. This particular team doesn't have a machine gunner who can lay down a carpet of covering fire when needed, does it?"

You know, I think she's right, Llenn realized.

Something she'd only learned after she started playing *GGO* was that in gunfights, the primary source of muscle for soldiers was a good old machine gun that could spray with speed and consistency, keeping the enemy trapped in place.

Holding the enemy down with a machine gun covering fire while agile riflemen circled around and picked them off from the side was a central pillar of tactical combat. Dealing with a machine gunner who could fire continuously was one-half of the nasty kind of enemy you didn't want to face. That was something Llenn came to understand very well, dealing with SHINC and ZEMAL. The other half was snipers who could put a bullet in any target, no matter how small.

Fukaziroh asked, "Pito, why don't you use that huge-ass gun you were blasting in the test session? It was like, boom, ka-bamm, ska-pow!"

Why is your vocabulary so limited?! Llenn thought but did not say aloud.

"What, the bazooka? It was fun to shoot, but it's not great for Squad Jam. Plus, you need someone else to reload it for you,"

Pitohui pointed out casually. "So anyway, from my massive gun collection, I will choose a machine gun that's been polished to a sheen but collecting dust—er, just an expression, really—and fire the hell out of it! You guys remember in elementary school how someone always had to be on machine-gun duty."

Uh, no, Llenn thought but did not say aloud.

"Oh yeah. I hated having to pick up the empty shells and clean the barrel when it was my turn," said Fukaziroh. Llenn ignored her.

Karen Kohiruimaki had gone to a different elementary school than Miyu Shinohara, though. So maybe Miyu's elementary school over in Obihiro had a 0.0001 percent chance of having a job in every class to take care of the machine gun.

"Just a minute. Wouldn't it be better if M had the machine gun, since he's the slowest?" Shirley asked. "A machine gunner doesn't need to move that quickly. And he can use his shield to set up a blind for defense. A different set of gear would allow you to make use of your speed better, Pitohui."

"I understand your logic, but it's not going to happen."

"Let's hear why not, then."

"Well, I was going to make a big, sensational splash of an announcement later, but oh well. You see, the truth is, in this event, M—and you won't believe this. Oh my gosh, it's gonna blow your mind—"

"It'll be faster just to show you," said M, cutting off Pitohui's time-wasting by waving his hand and opening his inventory. He began materializing items; motes of light gathered in the empty space before him, taking form as a thin but long, quite long, very long, extremely long gun.

"Oh! A new one? A new one?" Clarence's eyes sparkled.

"It's freakin' huge!" Fukaziroh blurted out. Llenn had the same thought but was able to hold herself back from saying anything.

The gun in the air was as long as a drying rod. M caught it in both hands, and you could tell that it took on weight by the way his arms tensed.

He had enough strength to handle it easily, though; his expression was cool as a cucumber as he placed it on the table with a bipod and a rear leg.

The gun's right-side bolt had been pulled open. It wouldn't fire at all in this state, so there was no fear of an accidental misfire. No one in *GGO* would complain about that sort of thing, but with real guns, it was always a matter of course that you safely disengaged the weapon like this.

There was now a massive gun over six feet in length on the round table. The front half of the gun was one long barrel. The rear half had a bolt-action mechanism that had to be manually operated between each shot, with a fat scope on top. There was an independent grip on the underside for use when shooting.

In the back, there was a sturdy stock and a single leg for planting into the ground. The whole weapon was a tan color. Only the scope was black.

"An antimateriel sniper rifle," Shirley murmured.

An antimateriel sniper rifle—or just "antimateriel rifle"—used huge bullets, much bigger than a normal sniper rifle's, that packed a devastating punch.

Despite the "antimateriel" description, it was totally normal to use them on people.

They were great in terms of power alone, but, of course, the guns were huge, heavy, and difficult to deal with.

"It looks like the gun SHINC has," Llenn observed.

In fact, it looked exactly the same size as the antimateriel PTRD-41 rifle, which they'd been using since SJ2. The PTRD-41 was called an antitank rifle, but only because that was the term for weapons like this around WWII, when it was developed. Nowadays, it would be filed under the antimateriel rifle category.

M said, "Two days ago, I finished a really difficult mission at last and earned this Ukrainian antimateriel rifle called the Alligator. It's exactly two meters long. Weighs fifty-five pounds. Fires 14.5 × 114 mm rounds, same as SHINC's antitank rifle. I mean, those bullets were developed specifically *for* that antitank rifle."

He pulled out an ammo container that looked like a gigantic lunch box, extracting suitably massive bullets as he explained the features of the gun. The bullets were about six inches long and looked big and sharp enough to stab a person, or to use as a bludgeon.

It was a major difference from Llenn's P90 ammo, which was barely the size of her pinkie. Still, if she put it right into the brain, a single one of those tiny bullets could easily kill a person, too. Bullets are scary.

"How far can you aim with it?" asked Shirley, who had a natural interest in sniping.

"I've been practicing nonstop with it since I got it. Against a nonmoving target with no wind, I can hit a human-sized target at two thousand meters. That's with no bullet line, of course. If I used one, I would guess I could go farther out."

"Talk about a monster..."

In the wide-open airport of SJ4, Shirley had made a successful snipe shot of over eleven hundred meters. That was her personal best.

But it was a hit on a trike, which was several times the size of a person. If you were trying to hit a person normally, eight hundred was the best you could do. Two thousand was just preposterous.

With bullets of this size, incidentally, any hit on the trunk of the body was instantly fatal. If you hit the head, everything above the neck would be blown off, and a hit to the torso could easily split the target in two.

"What did you mean, Shirley? Is the gun a monster? Or is M?" Clarence asked.

"Well, both," Shirley said honestly.

Even though it was a military weapon, which she had no interest in, this was quite a terrifying gun. If she used it to go hunting, there wouldn't be any meat left to eat on the kill. Maybe it would be useful for taking down a berserk African elephant if one ever started rampaging through town.

"So now M can perform ultra-long-range sniping just like SHINC, and attack buildings and vehicles! That's great to have!" Llenn raved.

It seemed to her that if M was using this as his second loadout weapon, then Pitohui would have to have the machine gun. It all made sense.

And she also realized SHINC would be doing the same thing.

In SJ1, Sophie had a PKM machine gun. But in SJ2, she gave up her gun in order to carry the PTRD-41 so that they had a weapon to break through M's shield.

This time, however, she could carry both of them, with one being for someone else. It could only serve to make the battles more white-knuckled.

"Well, it sounds like you two have your second loadouts settled," Clarence noted, Takarazuka features rounded with curiosity. "But what should Llenn and I, the peashooter duo, use for ours? It's nice to take the enemy by surprise, but I can't use something big and heavy."

Clarence and Llenn used different guns that had the same size bullets and magazines: 5.7 × 28 mm rounds. In other words, the diameter of the bullet was 5.7 mm, and the full length was 28 mm.

That was a very small bullet. Llenn's P90 was developed along with that bullet standard as an entirely novel specification, and Clarence's AR-57 was designed to make use of it later.

Assault rifles use rifle rounds, and submachine guns use pistol rounds. But these guns were designed to fill the gap between the two in terms of size and power.

These two girls had similar tactical styles, in that they used their agility as a weapon and fired many small bullets very quickly. But because of that, the girls' carrying capacity was low, and they wouldn't be able to hold a heavy machine gun and the ammo it needed to fire. Sniper rifles were a bit out of their range, too, because you either needed a lot of skill levels or a lot of real sniping skill.

But a lighter assault rifle that they could have carried wouldn't be much different from their current guns, eliminating the aspect of surprise. It would only increase their range and power slightly.

In that case, better to use the trusty guns they were familiar with already. They would be more accurate with them anyway, which, by definition, made them more powerful in combat.

M said, "I'd recommend a shotgun for you, Clarence. An automatic."

He waved a hand to summon his menu, then made a gesture like he was hurling something toward Clarence, who was sitting on the other end of the table. A window that was visible for everyone, not just M, slid over toward Clarence.

"Ohhh?"

It featured a list of automatic shotguns perfect for battle that could be purchased in *GGO*. It wasn't just a graphical list, either, but included caliber, magazine size, price, and weight. The shotguns were mostly for hunting, but some of them were for combat, too.

"You can manage that weight just fine, can't you?" asked M.

Clarence was slower than Llenn but could carry much, much

more. She gazed at the numbers and nodded. "Yeah. This seems good. I've made it this far without being able to hit distant targets anyway. Long live the shotgun! I'll get in some practice!"

The effective range of a shotgun varied wildly depending on the bullets used. A single-shot type could cover only about 150 yards. Standard shotguns for combat were even shorter, maybe fifty yards at best.

Instead, their power at close range was formidable. The 00 buck, which was good for combat, fired nine pellets of buckshot, each eight millimeters wide, in a single blast. When these were unleashed, spraying within a certain radius and hitting the target at the same time, a player in *GGO* suffered a momentary stun effect.

This was a deadly serious consequence. Even players with plenty of hit points left could easily die if hit by multiple shotgun blasts in a row.

"Good. If you have any questions about picking a gun, just ask me. Or message me. If you need more help, I can go shopping with you."

"Okay! I have a bunch of questions, but we can go shopping tomorrow or later. I want to go to bed early tonight. I'm logging off at nine o'clock, in thirty minutes. I'll try to do as much research as I can by tomorrow. What about you, Llenn? Gonna go with a shotgun, too?"

"Hmm," Llenn murmured, looking skeptically at the list of shotguns on the window. Most of them were long and thin.

Generally, shotguns came in the "magazine tube" style, with a tube about the same width below the barrel, where you inserted the rounds. If you increased the number of shots you could fire, for better use in combat, that also increased the length of the gun.

"I think these are too long for me to use."

"Ohhh."

"A more compact weapon would be better for your size, Llenn," said M.

"I get that, but that would mean another submachine gun like P-chan or a light assault rifle with a short barrel. And that's not surprising, is it? Plus, I already have the Vorpal Bunnies for handguns... Is there even anything worth using for a second loadout?"

"I've been thinking about the same thing. And I arrived at an answer. I used your previous Squad Jam experience as inspiration."

"And it is?"

"It is..."

M proceeded to answer Llenn's question. Their teammates exclaimed when they heard it, impressed.

When M was done, Llenn said, "Got it! I'll do that!"

She had no follow-up questions.

"Well, now that we've settled all of the second loadouts for the team..."

"Hold on, Pito... Are you doin' this on purpose...?"

"Oh my goodness, I completely forgot."

Of course it was on purpose. The only person whose second loadout hadn't been decided yet was Fukaziroh.

"Shouldn't Fuka just stick with what she's got now, like Shirley?" suggested Llenn.

Fukaziroh's weapons were MGL-140s, a pair of 40 mm six-shooter grenade launchers. That alone was a bizarre choice no typical player would ever think to choose.

No one could outdo her in terms of firepower. She was pure power, a real meathead. But she'd proven her worth in every battle so far, so there was no need to force her to change things up. Her skill at launching grenades into the distance was tremendous as it was.

But despite all this, Llenn couldn't help but think, *Knowing*

Fukaziroh, she's definitely going to want a second loadout. After all, it was just more fun that way.

"Nuh-uh! Nuh-uh! I'm gonna take a second loadout, too! It'll be way more fun that way!"

See? I knew it.

"If everyone else is getting a makeover, it's no fair if me and Shirley are the only ones who get left out!" said Fukaziroh with a pout.

"I don't actually care," said Shirley. "As long as you've mastered your way of fighting, that should be fine." It was hard to tell if she was scolding Fukaziroh for throwing a tantrum or offering an answer to make her feel better.

"Well, your dozen-grenade barrage is truly incredible. It's hard to come up with anything that can improve on power like that. What's the point of startling the enemy if it makes you weaker instead?"

"Not you, too, Pito!"

"Well, since they came up with this special rule, I suppose I understand why you'd want to have fun with the gear-switching system."

"That's better, Pito!"

"So what do you want, then?"

"If I knew that, I would tell you! C'mon, M, help me out. This is what you're here for, isn't it?"

"Hrmm..."

M's craggy face twisted in concentration. He really didn't know what to say.

"Fuka, you have high strength and stamina, so you could handle a very heavy weapon...but...while this is very difficult to tell you..."

"No! You don't need to spell it out! I know that my shooting ability leaves much to be desired! I suck! I knew it! Ugh!"

"Well, I wouldn't say it like *that*...but yes."

"So you *are* saying it!" fumed Fukaziroh. Yes, she was very bad at shooting guns.

The first gun she acquired in *GGO* was the ultraexpensive and heavy six-shooter grenade launcher—a gun most players would never experience, or *want* to experience. So Fukaziroh never went through the practice that every other player got with ordinary, basic guns, and she never picked up those skills.

For one thing, she totally skipped the intro and tutorial, assuming she didn't need them. This is not the sort of thing that a good player does.

On the plus side, however, she had gained much experience with shooting grenade launchers, which made her a very dangerous player to face.

"Geez, thanks a lot! So I'm just supposed to give up on having a second loadout?! Once you give up, your Squad Jam might as well be over!" She pouted, going into full-on tantrum mode. Shirley and Clarence both gave her a look that said, *What are we going to do with you?*

"Pito, M," Llenn said, for the sake of her friend and the team, "please, you have to—"

"Llenn! I knew you were my pal!"

"—convince her to give up."

"What?! Llenn! Come on!"

"Hrmm..." M's face was looking truly pained now. But after a couple of seconds, he said, "Oh, I thought of something."

"That's it!" exclaimed Fukaziroh, accepting the idea before she had even heard it.

Llenn turned to her. "You're sure?"

"If there isn't going to be any other answer, then the answer we do have is the best one! Once you've gone through some romantic relationships, you'll understand, Llenn."

"Do *not* talk to me about that right now."

"What does that mean? Are you a virgin in real life, Llenn?" asked Clarence with a smile. Llenn shot Shirley a look, asking her to take care of her partner, please. It was a pleading look. A look that said, *Kill her if you have to.*

"Awww, c'mon. It doesn't hurt to talk abou— *Mrrgbph!*"

The moment Shirley had gotten her hands around Clarence's mouth, Llenn used the opportunity to change the topic at light speed.

"What's the answer, M?"

M gave a brief explanation of his idea.

"Oh, I like it! That sounds best!" she exclaimed.

"Right?" said Fukaziroh.

At nine o'clock, Clarence said, "Oops, time's up. Time for beddy-bye. I'll log off first. See you tomorrow, M. Good night, everyone!" And she vanished in a puff of light, leaving just five of them in the private room.

The SJ5 preparation meeting was already over. They'd decided on the second loadouts for all members except Shirley, as well as who would carry each set.

Llenn's second loadout would be carried by her combat buddy, Fukaziroh, and vice versa. M and Pitohui would carry each other's. And naturally, Shirley would have Clarence's.

"Well, that all seems sensible. By the way," Shirley said, glaring at Pitohui, "when we split up after the start of SJ4, you said I could come after you if I wanted. Is that invitation still on the table, I assume?"

Pitohui paused in the act of consuming her mystery-colored drink and grinned at her. "You bet!"

"Very good. Then I'm looking forward to SJ5. I'll be practicing my shooting—to eliminate *you*."

And with a big smile, the lone-wolf sniper left the room like a sudden breeze, cool as you please.

Still holding the cup of iced coffee with no cream and extra syrup, because she hadn't finished it yet.

After Shirley left, the room settled into a proper lazy weekend mood, suitable for a Saturday night, only inside a game instead of real life.

"I just wanna enjoy a normal Squad Jam," Llenn grumbled sadly. She had been through more than enough to have earned the right to say this.

In SJ1, she was stuck in a two-man team with M, but it was a normal game at the start. However, despite their good pace taking down enemy teams, M dropped out partway, leaving her alone to rampage against a team of six. Although he did come back to save her at the very, very end.

In SJ2, the self-destructive urges of the face-tatted woman smirking right before her eyes put Llenn through hell. From start to finish, it was a mentally exhausting game. It was a good thing she was still here at all.

In SJ3, she thought she'd have a proper good time for once, but the stupid writer's crappy special rules put her through the wringer. Llenn had been the one chosen to be the team's betrayer, but because Pitohui (who wasn't chosen) ran off on her own, acting weird, the battle turned out even more chaotic than it should have been. At the time, Llenn decided that she needed to speak her mind clearly when the situation called for it. It was a learning experience for her.

In SJ4, thanks to Fire Nishiyamada, she was forced once again into a desperate, abnormal gameplay situation with consequences beyond her *GGO* life. And then she got dumped in real life. She didn't want to remember it. In fact, she completely forgot. What happened anyway?

"Oh, Llenn, this *will* be normal."

"I don't wanna hear it from you, Pito!"

"I'm guessing!"

"That's not helping!"

"Just forget your real-world troubles and unleash all your instincts for battle in this virtual world! Have fun with SJ5—it's just a game. A game where no one's going to die. Enjoy a good battle with your rivals or the pursuit of victory as a whole."

"Yeah, that was my plan..."

She'd already been playing *GGO* for over a year.

Her reason for starting was to become someone other than herself, a girl who was self-conscious about her tall height, and she felt like she'd accomplished that goal. She might have accomplished it *too* well.

She never would have guessed that she had such athleticism, such spirit, such determination, such an instinct to fight, or such a knack for slaughter.

She hoped her parents would never find out about it. She *really* hoped they never found out.

Llenn sighed and popped the straw of her iced tea into her mouth.

"Hmm?" Fukaziroh grunted softly but with real shock.

"Wzzup?" said Llenn, resting her chin on the table and pulling the cup sideways so she could keep the straw in her mouth. It was very bad posture—and all in the service of using as little energy as possible.

"I just got a message. It says, 'To all players who wish to take part in SJ5.'"

Apparently, she was looking at a window that was visible only to her.

"Uh-huh? What's it say?"

"Um, well, it's nothing really serious. I don't really know who sent it, either. It looks like a throwaway account."

"What? Are people sending spam in *GGO* now?"

"Based on the message, I think it's legit. Hmm. Well, it's not going to get sent to you, so you don't have to worry about it, I think."

Slurp, slurp, gulp.

Llenn sucked in a mouthful of iced tea and swallowed it. "Really? I dunno, now you're making me curious," she admitted.

"No, really, it's nothing big. All it says is that whoever eliminates Llenn in the next Squad Jam will be paid a hundred million credits, that's all."

"Ohhh."

She put her lips around the straw again, pulled a fresh swig of liquid into her mouth, and then spat it out spectacularly.

"Blrrrft!"

CHAPTER 2

Bounty, Thy Name Is Llenn

CHAPTER 2
Bounty, Thy Name Is Llenn

Twelve thirty PM, September 19th.

"Good day to everyone tuning in! We're here with the fifth Squad Jam, but you can simply call it SJ5! That's right, we love our guns, we love our mums, and this one goes out to all you bums!"

In the spacious main hall of a certain large bar in SBC Glocken, the starting point of Squad Jam, a man was screaming rhymes into a mic with extreme excitement.

"It's me again, your commentating gunfighter, Thane! Lately I've been getting barked at a lot by the dogs in my neighborhood!"

It was him.

Thane's avatar was of average height, average build, and average looks, but there wasn't a single person in this pub who didn't know who he was.

His videos were very highly regarded. They were far, far more entertaining than the official replays of the event, which picked up hardly any sound and consisted only of battle scenes. You didn't get bored watching Thane.

"Yeah! This is more like it!"

"Congrats on getting through the prelims!"

"Make it another fun one this time!"

"Hey, buddy! Try to last longer, why don't ya!"

"Yeah, you die too quickly all the time!"

"Show us more of the battle!"

"Team up with a much stronger squad for once!"

Excited and irresponsible cheers and jeers cascaded over him from the packed audience in the bar.

Thane's team, *Zangiri Atama no Tomo* (Close-Cropped Friends), abbreviated to ZAT, fell to MMTM in SJ2, SHINC in SJ3, and Llenn's team in SJ4 while they were distracted by monsters. In each case, it happened in the early stages. They got their asses kicked.

As a team, they had the talent to make it through the qualifying round each time, but not much further than that. There was a general, unspoken understanding among all that you shouldn't bring up the possibility that Thane's focus on live-commentating the event made him largely useless in battle.

"Thank you, everyone! Thank you, thank you! Yes, I suppose living longer is my goal for today! Maybe this gear-switch concept will make a difference this time. I hope it does. But I'll be ready for the worst, in any case. Aaaanyway, we've got thirty minutes left until the start of SJ5, and twenty until the cutoff to participate. This is about the time that all the teams come strolling into the bar! If I spot a well-known squad, I am going full-on journalism mode and charging in for some hard-hitting raw interviews!" he declared.

Just as he said that, the swinging double doors gave way, and a group of players walked through.

"Uh-oh! And here we have just such a team!"

Six men came into the bar—and just like that, it was silent.

To a man, they all wore Swedish army fatigues, a pattern of simple, straight lines in various hues of green. It was MMTM.

When not in tag form, their official name was Memento Mori, a famous Latin phrase meaning "Remember you must die." The patches on their shoulders bore the insignia of a skull with a knife in its mouth.

Their leader, David, and the rest of the members were extremely talented soldiers. Most of all, their skill was in their teamwork. They were never simply working alone.

In all honesty, you could say they were the top team in Squad Jam, in terms of overall team ability, but for some reason, their survival rate was poor. They had never won the event.

Maybe they were just unlucky because they kept having to face Llenn and Pitohui. Naturally, MMTM's hatred of Llenn and Pitohui was deeper than the ocean, and beating them to win was the majority of their motivation.

"The first through the door are MMTM! The championship favorites who've never been champions! I'll go and get a word from them!" Thane said, rushing toward the team as they made their way for the private rooms at the back of the bar.

"Hello!" he said as loud as he could.

Kshing! David fixed him with a malevolent stare.

"That's all I wanted to say!" Thane claimed, and returned just as quickly.

"What the hell was that?!"

"What a wuss!"

"Go in there and get killed!"

"Where's your pride as a journalist?!"

"Don't chicken out!"

"Don't be afraid!" the audience jeered.

But they didn't know what it was like.

Just as MMTM left the main hall, another group of six slipped inside.

"Oh?"

Thane and all the others looked their way, but nobody recognized the men. They'd never even seen them on a video stream. Were these newcomers to the event? Probably.

So when another team entered the door behind them, all eyes slid over to them, and the bar promptly erupted into sound at the sight of the six women.

"Uh-oh, here they are! The Amazons! In SJ3…you were a big help!" Thane said, ignoring the first team and slipping past them.

As it happened, the first six were T-S, the champions of SJ2.

Without their full-body armor and helmets, nobody realized who they were. Fortunately for them, this meant they could simply sit at one of the tables in the hall, rather than needing a private room.

Thane sidled up to SHINC as they made their way through the bar. "Hello, ladies! You're all looking lovely today, let's say for the sake of argument!" he said obsequiously, preparing to get hit.

But the pigtailed gorilla in the lead simply grinned at him. "Hey there, combat cameraman. You haven't learned your lesson yet, huh? I'll have to kill you again—in SJ, of course."

"Heh. I'd like to…see you try," Thane said as bravely as he could manage. He did earn some laughs for that one. At least, the Amazons in SHINC laughed.

They were heading for a private room in the back, but Thane tagged along next to them. "How do you feel about your chances today?"

"Well, it should be interesting…but it'll be the same as always. We'll give it everything we've got," Boss said tantalizingly.

"I've got high hopes! You are certainly a team with the potential to win it all! Even if you haven't!" he said, which sounded like a taunt.

"I'll take that as a compliment," she replied, taking the high road. "I'm noticing you're not sexually harassing us today."

"Huh? Did you want me to?"

"So I can sue you?"

"I'm sorry! Just one final question, if you'll allow me! It's a real serious question, of course!"

They were almost to the private rooms now. Boss said, "What?"

"The special rules this time allow for a secondary gear loadout, right? I assume you've come prepared with your own?"

"Of course. We don't believe our opponents will be easy enough to let us win without it."

"And...what exactly is your secondary gear?"

"The point is to use it to surprise your opponents. Do you really think I'll say it here?"

"Please, anything you can tell my viewers," Thane persisted with a smile.

"Fine, I'll tell you. I've brought along a sexy bikini that'll blow your mind," she said, gorilla features smiling at the obvious joke.

Thane suddenly looked somber and switched to a serious reporter's tone. "And that was her answer, which leaves us with more questions than when we began. Back to you in the studio."

"Hey, shut up!"

"All right, Boss, enough playing around. Let's go," said Sophie, prodding her on the back. Boss and the others vanished into the private room.

Once they were gone, Thane said, "Oh, shoot!" as he remembered something. "I forgot to ask them about their friend, the little pink demon, having a hundred-million-credit bounty on her head!"

Minutes later, after a number of nameless teams had passed through and found seats throughout the bar, Thane's eyes lit up.

"Oh, here we go! At last! I had a feeling they'd show up! It's the defending champions! Out of respect for their accomplishment, I will call them by their full, official name, not the tag sign! It's the All-Japan Machine-Gun Lovers!"

"Whoaaa!"

"They're here!"

"I'm so excited!"

"Congrats on winning it all!"

"Open bolts!"

The audience in the bar, having swelled over time, was exuberant.

Thane's commentary was equally excited. "They suffered hardly any damage and lost not a single member in SJ4! Aside from the team that took advantage of circumstances in SJ2, no one's had a cleaner win than them! That's ZEMAL! Remember that name, because I surely will! And by the way, I pronounce that tag *Zee-mall*, not *Zem-mal*. Is that okay? Sorry if I've been doing it wrong!"

As Thane said, in SJ1 they were pushovers who got easily taken out from behind while they were having fun shooting at Llenn, and now they were champions. If you wanted to call them the team that had grown the most in the history of Squad Jam, you weren't wrong.

Last time, they'd entered the bar with their new member, the only girl in the group, hoisted on their shoulders. But having won, they received prize money and a modicum of good sense, because they were walking in like normal people this time.

There was no question that Vivi was their leader, and it was clear to everyone that her arrival to the team launched ZEMAL into the stratosphere. All of their strategies in SJ4 had come from her, surely.

Thane said, "Excuse me, goddess of machine guns!" as he barreled into view.

The men in ZEMAL did not protest at the mention of the word *goddess*. They were her believers. They agreed with him.

"You were tremendous in SJ4! I was amazed! I'm looking forward to another complete and total victory today!"

"Thank you. We'll do our best to live up to expectations," Vivi said with a dazzling smile, sending the room into a frenzy.

For one thing, *GGO* had very few female players. And the ones you found in Squad Jam were vicious pip-squeaks, or wicked face-tattooers, or gorilla Amazons, or murderous snipers, or boyish temptresses. In other words, all insane—er, unique and quirky types. But Vivi was different.

Between her attitude, her manners, and the fact that she would paint a very pretty picture in an office setting with a change of outfits, she was altogether a very fetching grown woman.

Thane simpered a bit and said cheerily, "There's a special set of rules around gear-switching this time, but given how you make full use of the machine gun's qualities, you might need it, wouldn't you say?"

"Perhaps. But maybe we've got something up our sleeves."

"Well, you'd hope to startle your opponents, wouldn't you? And speaking of surprises, there's that strange bounty going around," remarked Thane, asking the question he failed to pose to SHINC. "Are you going to keep an eye out for that?"

Vivi considered this for a moment. "The pink demon is referring to Llenn, I presume. I've heard about it, but I don't know how much to trust it," she said without interest—or without letting on her interest, at least.

But Thane persisted. "You didn't hear the rest? The hundred million credits are already on display on the SJ5 bulletin board as an item within an item box. Once you've fulfilled the bounty, the winner will get sent the code to unlock it and claim the prize!"

This display was set up right after the bounty message was sent out.

In order to prevent fraudulent dealings, it was impossible to falsify the contents of an item box. The amount of money contained inside it was as real as real could be in this game.

Whether or not the player who eliminated Llenn would actually receive the code in a DM was a different matter.

"Oh, I didn't know that," said Vivi, whose dazzling smile made it impossible to tell if she was telling the truth or not. She continued, "In Squad Jam, every other team is your enemy. If you see them, you beat them. That includes the pink demon, of course. If we happen to earn something for doing that, I suppose I'd gladly take it. So long."

The interview was over. Peter slid in between the two, playing the role of bodyguard.

"I'm looking forward to seeing your results!" said Thane, withdrawing willingly.

In VR worlds like *GGO*, there were sixty seconds for each actual minute of time.

The second hand on the clock in the pub ticked slowly onward as various teams made their way inside. Thane commentated on each entrance, keeping the crowd engaged. The only major difference this time was the lack of the mysterious masked squads in a tag-team alliance.

One forty-five PM passed, then 1:46, then 1:47, and at two minutes to go, the crowd got restless.

"They're not here yet."

"Yeah..."

"We didn't miss them, did we...?"

"I don't think so..."

The two-time champion of SJ1 and SJ3 (and thus leader in that category) and pink-clad pip-squeak was nowhere to be found; neither was her team. If no part of their bodies entered the bar by 12:50, they would be disqualified from SJ5 for being late.

"Probably waiting until the last moment again." They'd barely made it in SJ2 and SJ3.

"What if they're already here? Like that other time."

In SJ4, it seemed like they didn't show up, but they'd actually been waiting in a private room since an hour beforehand, so some people guessed it was that trick again.

"Nah. I've been here for four hours, and I haven't seen a single member of the pink devil's team yet," someone said, to the shock of those who heard it.

"No way..."

"When are you showing up, Llenn...?"

"C'mon, man..."

"Why were *you* here so early, actually?"

"Ever since I lost my job, my wife bugs me about being at home. I had to escape to a Net café."

"Thanks for that brutally honest story."

Then someone noticed a new team coming in. "Oh, who's that...? Huh?"

Thane also muttered, "What the—?"

"Huh?"

"Whut?"

"Why?"

The entire audience inside the bar was quite shocked by what they saw.

It was the group they'd been waiting for: Team LPFM, with M towering in the lead.

But there were two things that shocked the onlookers.

"The pink devil isn't here… Oh no! Why? Qué pasa?!" Thane jabbered. Indeed, there were only five of them.

Massive M, tattooed Pitohui, tiny grenadier Fukaziroh, explosive sniper Shirley, and handsome girl Clarence.

One, two, three, four, five. That was it, nothing more.

No Llenn.

Perhaps she was just in the back because she was so small, they wondered. But it was not so. She wasn't there. Simply absent. Not following in the others' footsteps.

"And what's going on with them? They're all carrying their guns in the open! A little early for that, isn't it, guys? You gonna stick up this tavern? And, M…what is *that* thing, man?!" Thane jabbered. Indeed, all five were fully equipped, from guns to protective vests to helmets to holsters to backpacks. They were wearing what they'd have on in Squad Jam.

There wasn't any reason you *couldn't* do this—but it wasn't typical.

Trotting along at the front was Fukaziroh, MGL-140s hanging off both shoulders, while Pitohui held a KTR-09 in her right hand. Shirley and Clarence had their primary weapons in slings on their backs, too.

But the big surprise was M.

He was holding his brand-new antimateriel rifle, the Alligator, right out in the open, just showing it off to everybody.

A giant at six feet tall, holding a rifle like a six-foot spear on his right shoulder, stomping through the room. On his back was the huge pack he always carried, with the unbeatable defensive shield folded inside it.

The team was fully armed in a way you'd see only during Squad Jam and with some brand-new gear, to boot. He was carrying around the powerful gun that should have been a surprise for their hapless opponents.

"What the hell is that…?"

"That's…an Alligator antimateriel rifle! They put it in the game…?!"

"There's a lot more antimateriels now. You just don't see them in the stores yet."

"Because they'd sell out the instant they appear."

"They're saying if you want one, you gotta beat some mega-hard quests."

"I just started playing *GGO*, and I don't know the first thing about guns…but is that a Ukrainian bolt-action rifle with a five-shot 14.5 × 114 mm magazine?"

"Sounds like you know plenty."

"It's huge. Though it looks a bit smaller when M's carrying it."

"Thing's a lance. You could kill someone just by holding it at your side and charging with it."

"If I held that thing upright at my house, it would jab straight through the ceiling. I'd never get my security deposit back."

"Okay, enough real-world talk."

While the patrons of the bar added their own unnecessary commentary, Thane did the same. "A mystery! What a mystery! This ordinary, unremarkable *Gun Gale Online* bar has suddenly been plunged into the world of mystery! And to solve this mystery, special agent Thane has stifled the terror rising from his gut to proceed into the heart of mystery itself!"

He crossed the floor to the armed group, who were proceeding as slowly as a daimyo's procession, and for some bizarre reason, asked in English, "H-hello! Everybody! How you doing?"

"Why English?" Fukaziroh replied in kind, lifting her helmeted head to glance at Thane.

Without missing a beat, he said, "Because I can't speak French!"

"That makes sense," said Fukaziroh, satisfied with his answer.

She continued walking, as if to say that Thane's job was done for now. Her face was determined, and her steps were firm, regal, and teensy.

Left behind, Thane turned to Pitohui next. "Ma'am, ma'am! Please, just two questions! Two is all I need! There's no time, so I'll just ask them! Where's the pink pip-squeak? And why are you all weapon exhibitionists?"

The tattooed woman said casually, "Llenn decided not to attend."

It was as casual as if she'd said, *For breakfast this morning, I had toast with strawberry jam, plus natto and foie gras.*

"Wha—?! Whaaat?!" he screamed, and a shriek-like ripple ran through the audience in the room.

Just then, a woman's voice began the announcement that participants would soon be teleported to the waiting room, but the murmuring was so loud that no one could hear it.

Pitohui spoke as she walked, as if this wasn't really such a strange thing. "As you all know, poor Llenn has some weird bounty on her head. She started sulking and said, 'This is stupid. Stop ruining my Squad Jam. I'm not going to play. Good luck, everyone.' We just got her private messages a little while ago. We told her it was just a game, and asked her to come and have fun with us, but oh well. Sorry if you were looking forward to seeing her. The five of us will be fine, though. We've got a new weapon, too. I'm guessing we'll probably win this time, yet again. So long."

As she walked off, Thane stopped in his tracks and murmured, "Oh my God..."

In the silence that followed, the stately procession continued out of the hall and into a private room.

Back on his own, Thane returned to his senses and announced, "D-did you all hear that? Did you hear that? What a shocker! A huge surprise! The pink shrimp is not taking part! Holy crap! A bolt from the blue! A twist of fate! What about the bounty?! What about SJ5?!" he screamed theatrically before realizing something. "Oh, wait. She didn't say why their weapons are out."

And then it was 12:50.

Like all the other participating players, Thane vanished from the spot, sent to the ten-minute waiting area.

The waiting area was dark and cramped.

If you weren't standing on it, you wouldn't even be sure there was a floor underneath. There was just a floating display reading TIME REMAINING: 09:59, which proceeded to count down in silence.

This was time for the SJ participants to spend freely, perhaps checking and prepping their gear, or getting hyped or relaxed, or coming up with team strategies or not, or even just sitting around feeling bored.

It was also the place where players who died in Squad Jam were sent again to wait for ten minutes.

Fukaziroh muttered, "We totally fooled them," looking up at the mountain of a man who was her teammate. On M's back, the massive, camo-pattern backpack opened on its own.

"Bwah!"

A small pink-clad player popped her head out. It was Llenn, of course. She'd been huddled up the whole time, hiding in the backpack without so much as twitching a finger.

M explained, "The teams we fight will notice right away, but we can just take them out as quickly as possible. If the folks in the pub see on the screen, they have no way of telling the other players. At the very least, this should mean we won't get singled out by any teams who are just trying to play long enough to snag the bounty and don't care about winning. Veterans aside, any teams who were staking out the main room in hopes of getting intel are bound to be disappointed now."

Meanwhile, Llenn worked her top half out of the pack and wriggled up onto M's shoulders. She had removed all her gear for size reasons, so she was wearing only her pink fatigues. Once her legs were free of the bag, she hopped down and landed safely.

"Oh! You're here, Llenn? Oh no… I think I just lied to a journalist!" Pitohui exclaimed facetiously.

"Well, you were the one who told me to do it." Llenn glared at her. Yep, it was all *her* idea.

Pitohui smirked, warping her cheek tattoos. "The majority are going to think you're not here now, and they'll freak out when they see you. Like you're a ghost! Wow, what a brilliant idea… Sometimes I'm afraid of my own genius…"

"Yeah, yeah… Besides, I'm not going to skip out on Squad Jam just because of a stupid bounty." Llenn pouted, puckering her lips.

The tattoos warped even harder. "That's my Llenn!"

"I'm not yours, Pito."

Clarence was seated flat on the floor with her legs splayed out in front of her: total relaxation mode. "Hey, Llenn, are you *sure* you don't know who it is?" she asked.

Clarence was dressed in black from head to toe and had black hair, as well, which made her look like nothing more than a floating face in the black space. It was kinda freaky.

"No! I said no, already!"

The image of Fire Nishiyamada briefly flitted through Llenn's head, but she banished it. She had nothing more than intuition in this case, but it didn't seem like something he would do.

And through messages after the bounty announcement, Miyu and Goushi and Elza all agreed: This wasn't his work.

She asked Miyu why she'd come to that conclusion in a split

second. Her friend replied, "Probably because he doesn't want to have anything to do with you anymore."

Well, that truth bomb shut her up.

Llenn's answer to Clarence: "Well, if I had a hunch of who did it, it would be anyone I've killed in *GGO* and Squad Jam!"

"Ahhh, I see. But that's kind of an abnormal amount of money to put up just like that. It's weird. Like, obsessive-weird."

Credits in *GGO* could be converted to electronic cash. In other words, a real money transaction, or RMT. The exchange rate was 100:1, so one hundred million credits would be one million yen. In terms of cash to be spending on in-game entertainment, it was a bit bonkers.

"Well…I bet they all chipped in, bit by bit, and saved up the dough! Slow and steady!"

"I'm not sure about that…"

Even then, you'd be talking about a whoooole bunch of people who hated her, but why couldn't that be the case? Just ignore the rest of the logic that said it was unlikely.

"Now, now, Clare, we're not going to find out the answer just by debating it among ourselves," Pitohui cautioned her.

And when she noticed that Llenn was giving her the coldest, most wintry stare of suspicion possible, Pitohui added, "Let me be clear, once again, and say that it was not me!"

Seven days earlier, just after the bounty was put on Llenn's head, she got a message from SHINC's Boss, also known as Saki Nitobe.

It was an extremely long and impassioned message, but the point of it was rather simple.

In short: "This is messed up! Next Squad Jam, let's fight together until only our two teams are left!"

Llenn shared the contents of the message with her teammates, none of whom objected to the idea. They'd cooperated in SJ4 and the more recent quest, and there was no rule that favorites couldn't team up with each other.

Why not do it? Once they'd eliminated all other teams, they could split up and have another showdown.

But there was one big problem…

"In order to group up with SHINC, we'll have to wait for the 1:10 scan to determine their location and then leave it up to fate," M said when there were six minutes remaining in the countdown.

He had already put the Alligator back into item storage and given his gear-switching set, or alternate loadout, or second load-out, to Pitohui to carry.

Resting against his thick legs at the moment was his favorite 7.62 × 51 mm NATO-round-shooting battle rifle, the M14 EBR.

Inside the backpack where Llenn had been hiding was now the folded-up shield that had played such a huge role in past Squad Jams. Minutes earlier, only two pieces had been in the backpack to keep its structure. Llenn had been packed between them, like the filling of a shield sandwich.

Pitohui and the others had entered the bar decked out in their full starting gear already, so they had nothing to do.

Llenn, too, had her beloved P-chan in her hand and three ammo magazines on either hip, ready to go.

Between the seven in the pouches and the gun, plus everything packed into her inventory, Llenn had twenty-five magazines in total. That was 1,250 bullets. That was quite a lot—a feat made possible by small ammo and fifty-shot magazines.

Her combat knife, Kni-chan, was also in place behind her lower back.

She'd already received the Satellite Scan terminal, a crucial part of Squad Jam, and had it tucked into the shirt pocket of her combat outfit.

She also had the three thick pen-shaped "emergency med kit" items—the only healing item allowed in the event, for the sake of fairness—in a waist pouch in front, where they were easily reachable.

As always, the large jewellike anti-optical defensive field, which greatly decreased the amount of damage taken from optical guns, was fixed to her belt.

"Indeed, the rest is up to fate. It's the only way," said Fukaziroh, who was even more relaxed than Clarence, nearly to the point of falling asleep, her limbs fully splayed out, lying flat on her back.

Her pillow was a backpack stuffed with grenades. Her large green helmet was resting on top of her stomach.

Now that they were in agreement to fight alongside SHINC, the biggest problem was how they could find each other and meet up as soon as possible.

The previous standard had been to scatter the most powerful teams' starting points to the four corners of the map, which would presumably hold true here, too.

Those four teams would be ZEMAL, SHINC, MMTM, and Llenn's team. Each of them had started in a different corner in SJ4.

The game map would be a square exactly 10 kilometers to a side, a bit over 6 miles. In other words, the total size was 100 square kilometers. And by comparison, the Yamanote Line loop around Tokyo had an interior size of 63 square kilometers.

That was big. Very big. It was difficult for two teams to reach each other.

You couldn't set up your comm to patch in to enemy teams at

the start. You could only find them in person and connect them that way.

After the first Satellite Scan ten minutes into the game, the teams' locations would be revealed, but until that point, you couldn't take any reckless actions.

After that, you would have to cross the map, littered with enemies at the start, and find each other. Until then, they'd have to fight powerful opponents like MMTM and ZEMAL, and survive to meet up.

Whichever spot would be quickest to meet, whether that was the middle of the map (from opposite corners) or right along one of the sides of the map, was unknown for now. They couldn't do anything until 1:10, and then it would be up to fate.

"Llenn," said Shirley, who rarely spoke to others first. "I'm along on this trip now. I'll stay with you until we meet up with SHINC."

"Thanks! That's a huge help!" Llenn said, heartened.

"So will I, then!" said Clarence.

"Thanks!" Llenn replied.

"Don't be fooled, Llenn," drawled Fukaziroh, her eyes closed in an imitation of sleep. "They're just making up a convenient, self-serving reason for hanging with us because they know survival will be hard with just the two of them at the start."

"I know that! I've been competing in Squad Jams for years, now! But even if that's the case, I'm thankful because it increases the chances that *I* survive!"

"You're too nice for your own good, girlie. And that's one of your better qualities. But before we go on, folks, I just have one question I hope to get answers for…"

Without getting up, Fukaziroh continued, "Once our victory in SJ5 is all but confirmed—meaning when our cooperation with SHINC is over, and we've finished off all other teams—the only thing left will be to twist those girls' heads off. And assuming that's something we can easily do without you..."

"I know, Fuka! You don't have to spell it all out," said Pitohui gleefully.

"I know what you're about to say, too. I've been thinking about it this whole time," Clarence said, grinning.

Shirley probably knew as well but didn't say anything. M, as usual, was quiet.

Fukaziroh considered her horrifying speech.

"In that case, if I or our other teammates happen to shoot and punch and stab and kill you from behind...do you think we'd be eligible to receive the hundred-million credit bounty?"

"What?!"

Llenn, the one person who *didn't* know what Fukaziroh was going to say, did a spit take.

She came to the sudden, sweat-trickling realization that her teammates—Pitohui, Clarence, Shirley, and even Fukaziroh on the ground—were staring at her with a gleam in their eyes.

You could practically see the yen symbol in their pupils.

"H-h-h-hey! Y-you guys...you guys don't want money *that* bad, do you?!" she cried, a question straight from the soul.

"I do."

"I do."

"I do."

"I do."

Four voices spoke in order.

A moment later, M's deep voice added, "If they'll give it to me, I do, too."

Llenn shivered. It was a high-speed bodily vibration, made possible by her incredible agility stat.

"Grr, grrrrr...fine! If you're gonna try that, you better attack me all at once! I'll fight you all off! But only once our victory is all but guaranteed!"

"Okay," said Fukaziroh.

"You got it!" said Clarence.

"Will do," said Shirley.

"Roger that!" said Pitohui.

"Understood," said M, all in order.

The real strength of Team LPFM's bonds was that it was expected that the members would fight. Probably.

With this heartwarming thought in mind, the countdown proceeded until it hit one minute.

"All right, you goons, the bus to the battlefield is leaving! You got your tickets? Don't be late!" taunted Pitohui, pulling the loading lever of her KTR-09 to send the first bullet into the firing chamber. It made a nice metallic sound, the kind of thing that got every player in *GGO* pumped.

"Here we go, Rightony and Leftania..."

Fukaziroh hopped up to her feet, put on her helmet, and picked up the two MGL-140s she'd left on the ground.

"Hmm, I wonder what fun ways I'll get to kill someone this time. Viva murder!" Clarence beamed, loading her AR-57.

"Hope you're ready for your doom, Pitohui," Shirley said to her teammate, cycling the bolt on her R93 Tactical 2. The rifle featured a straight pull bolt, meaning you only had to go back and forth. It was nice and quick.

Then she flipped on the safety switch behind the bolt.

The only people in *GGO* who bothered to use the safety on their guns were people with actual firing experience in real life, because it was already an ingrained habit. That held true whether it was live ammo guns or airsoft.

But people who'd only ever shot guns in *GGO* never used the safety. They prioritized being able to shoot at any moment, and in a sense, this wasn't the wrong thing to do.

"Let's do our best. Switch to your second loadout as the situation demands. You don't need to wait for my orders," said M. He pulled and released the charging handle of the M14 EBR.

The piece of metal picked up the top bullet in the magazine and pushed it into the gun, producing a high-pitched click that was the most impressive of any of them.

Then M engaged the safety. He didn't forget.

The clock read five seconds left.

"Do your worst! Come one and come all! Try to take me out!"

The instant Llenn let go of the P90's loading lever, everyone around her turned into flashes of light, leaving no one behind in the darkened space.

Then, just as the countdown on the wall reached zero, large words appeared next to them.

They said, *About the special rules of SJ5: Here's more! It's really important! Read carefully! And don't give up, even if you die!*

They were followed by quite a long text explanation.

But there was no one there to actually read the text…

…*yet.*

CHAPTER 3
Alone in the Mist

CHAPTER 3
Alone in the Mist

As the flash of the teleportation effect faded, Llenn opened her eyes.

"Hmm?"

And it was still white all around.

In fact, it was a very light gray, or perhaps a milky white. It wasn't bright, but it was so uniform that she couldn't really see anything.

"Huh?"

For a moment, she thought the teleportation had failed. But that didn't happen in the VR world, so this was something else at play.

Without panicking or fretting, Llenn worked to understand the situation. She spun around in a full circle to see if anything different turned up.

"It's all white…"

There was nothing but white in all directions, as far as the eye could see. She looked up, too—still white.

Looking down, she saw her pink legs and a concrete surface. It was a bit hazy, but the substance was white concrete, a fairly common texture in *GGO*.

A few seconds later, understanding arrived.

"Ohhh, it's mist…"

She was surrounded by a very dense mist. That was why she couldn't see anything but her own feet.

Since the ground was white concrete itself, there was actually no way for her to tell exactly how far her visibility went.

If the waiting room was dark and mysterious, she'd been taken somewhere white and mysterious instead.

Maybe she could at least tell the directions. She looked up at the compass, which was always displayed directly overhead within the player's field of view.

"Awww, darn..."

But it wasn't working. The display was covered with a pale-red filter that blocked it out.

Depending on the map you were in, you might experience this effect elsewhere in *GGO*: The compass was unusable here.

There were various reasons the administrators gave for this—the damaged magnetic field was having an anomaly, magnetic waves put off by certain enemies were jamming the compass, and so on.

In short: *It doesn't work here because we say so, now shut up.*

"Hey, Llenn, where are you right now? You're too small for me to see you."

"Fuka?"

Her voice was only coming into Llenn's left ear—meaning it was through the comm. Because Llenn had the comm set to feed into her left ear. Explanation over. Also, you can use it in the right ear, or both, if you want.

Her teammates should have been teleported close by, so if she wasn't hearing the voice in her right ear, meaning it wasn't coming from the physical space nearby, that was a little strange.

"How can I tell you where I am? It's all mist around me. I can't see a thing to describe to you."

"Oh, me too. What about the others? M, Pito, Clare, Shirl, in that order," Fukaziroh instructed.

M's voice came back, also through the comm: "I'm also in very thick mist. I can't see where I am at all."

Then Pitohui: "Can't see a damn thing."

Then Clarence: "Same! It's like clouds. Geez, this is scary! By the way, what's the difference between mist and clouds?"

Lastly, Shirley: "Mist and clouds are basically the same thing. The only difference is whether it's touching the ground or up in the sky. It's rather spectacular mist, though. You couldn't even drive in this."

"Oh, I see. But even if it were totally clear, you probably shouldn't be driving anyway, Shirley," said Clarence.

"Forget about that right now," said Shirley, who could do just about anything…well, except drive a car.

"What do we do? Where are you guys…?" Llenn fretted. It appeared that she was somewhat distant from her teammates, but which direction should she go to find them?

It was better not to move about too recklessly, she decided. Especially because she was so fast and small.

"Wait," said M, his voice uncharacteristically concerned. "I'll ask each of you in turn. What's the ground beneath your feet like? Pito?"

"It's dark, damp earth."

"Shirley?"

"Hard, packed snow. Why, are you not standing in snow?"

"Clarence?"

"Huh? What are you guys talking about? I'm standing on dry, brown dirt! There's no snow at all!"

"Fuka?"

"I'm in a place with train tracks laid over gravel. It's one of those switchyards. The kind we saw at the start of SJ3. They're reusing their map data, lazy bastards."

"Llenn?"

"It's plain white concrete! Like a garage…or a road!"

This is crazy, Llenn thought but did not say aloud.

Everyone was standing on a different surface. If they had all been teleported to the same location, that shouldn't have been possible.

Which meant there was only one explanation.

"Do you mean…?"

If the information was correct, then the answer had to be, too, no matter how difficult it was to believe. Llenn spoke her conclusion out loud.

"We've all been teleported to different places?"

"That's right," M said with great finality. "We ended up in separate places. Or should I say, we were *sent* to them."

Sent? she wondered, right as the clock hit 1:03.

At that very moment, as though designed to arrive the second the mystery was solved, a message appeared.

Large black letters appeared against the white mist, an effect that only the player present could see.

The message was as follows.

Announcing more special rules!

I've scattered all team members at the start of the game! First things first: Good luck getting back together.

We have 180 players, after all, so you'll find enemies fairly close at hand. Be careful.

Only the team leaders, as the rules have always been, are kept at least two-thirds of a mile separate from any others.

Also, the mist will slowly clear up over time—very slowly.

But it will be totally clear by two o'clock, after an entire hour. So don't worry.

Your compass will be totally useless until then, however.

Also, you won't be able to see your teammates' hit points. The only indicator you will receive is an X mark over their name if they die.

On top of that! From the first Satellite Scan at 1:10 until the mist totally clears at two o'clock, your ability to use your comms will be interrupted. Until you actually meet up in person, you will no longer be able to contact your distant teammates.

Better figure out a plan now while you can still talk, huh?

"Huh?"

Llenn's jaw dropped—as did over a hundred other players' at the same time.

That goddamn sponsor was messing with the rules again, making life harder for everyone else. And without any warning ahead of time. Screw you, pal!

In *GGO* and other games, it was possible sometimes to get teleported somewhere in the game and find that you were separated from the rest of your party. It happened in the quest the other day.

And that certainly wasn't uncommon with misty areas like this one.

It was a trick that made enemy encounters thrilling and created a general sense of dread for players to enjoy.

The mist was something needed to make the most out of the rules, so useful items like night-vision goggles, infrared displays, and thermal goggles were certain to be useless here.

Still, you'd never guess that such a situation would arise in a team battle-royale event. With the added bonus of a disabled compass and the inability to communicate with your companions until you found one another.

M said, "I had a feeling it was something like this. Everyone, crouch down and make as little noise as possible. If you can use white camo, put it on now. Especially Llenn."

"G-got it..."

Llenn sat as quickly as a dog seeing its favorite treat in its owner's hand and brought up her inventory with a swipe of her left hand. She selected a snowy camo poncho of faded white with bits of gray smudging, materialized it, and put it on.

Her usual clothes stood out against anything but reddened desert sand, so she made sure to keep a stock of ponchos in various colors.

You want me to stop wearing pink? You might as well ask me to die!

The little pink frog crawling along the ground turned into a spotted white-and-gray frog. Shirley, meanwhile, did the same thing as soon as she'd confirmed her location. Those were sniper instincts at work.

"There's a good chance you have an enemy lurking within a hundred yards," M warned. Since it was through the comm, everyone could hear it clearly, even if he was muttering so quietly you wouldn't be able to hear him from two feet away. "Stay on highest alert. Rely on your ears. Make as little noise as possible from this point on."

Well, that made sense. You had up to 180 players, now spread out across a map exactly a hundred square kilometers in size.

The biggest official event in *Gun Gale Online*, the solo battle-royale event called the Bullet of Bullets, featured a map the same size with only thirty players. So this was an extremely chaotic adaptation of that format. What now?

Llenn's mind was awash with various thoughts, but she didn't say any of them out loud so as not to interrupt M's warnings.

"There's no use getting mad about these rules. We just have to do our best, no matter the circumstances. The first step is getting everyone back together. Whichever teams reunite safely are going to have a major advantage; they'll bc able to use their second loadouts, too. Make sure you all have your Satellite Scanners out, and hide the screen when you look at it."

Llenn did as he said. You had to hide the screen to keep the light from being visible at a distance. She used her right hand to cover the screen of the Satellite Scanner, a smartphone-like device, in her left hand. It displayed a map.

In previous Squad Jams, it would show a detailed terrain map, only indicating your own location at the start.

"Huh?"

There was a map here. But she couldn't see it.

It was completely white, to the point that she almost thought the screen was bugged-out. Like it was bought brand-new and had a piece of white printer paper stuck to the front.

And because she was the team leader, she would have normally expected to see her location on the map as a glowing white dot. She squinted, examining the screen closely, and after much effort, spotted something. There was a darker white dot, slightly different than the shade of the screen.

But since she couldn't see any details on the screen, she couldn't tell where she actually was. She could spread and pinch her fingers to zoom the map in and out, but the only thing it showed was a white dot on a white screen.

"I can't tell," she murmured to herself.

Her teammates had the same result. "This is no good," Fukaziroh muttered into her ear.

"I'm just guessing," Pitohui said to the group, "that we aren't going to be able to see the entire map until the mist is clear. There's a white dot for the leader's position on your screen, right, Llenn? Can you zoom in as far as you can?"

"Got it."

She did as she was asked and zoomed in farther than she'd done on her own. Her fingers repeated the pinch-out motion several times until it stopped working.

"I'm at max zoom. Nothing's any different," she reported. The screen was still all white.

"Now, be mindful of your surroundings and move a little bit. Like twenty yards, that's all."

"A-all right..."

Without understanding what this was accomplishing, Llenn rose to a crouch and quickly zipped forward over the ground. She was scuttling, like a certain flat, blackish, shiny insect that wasn't found in Hokkaido and whose name you would not want to think about.

The white ground underneath her scrolled past, until a broken white line appeared, marking the boundary between lanes. She was indeed on a very wide road, an expressway, perhaps.

"Oh!"

There was a change in the map. While it previously looked like a blank sheet of paper, there was now actual map there. It was a line of detail that looked like a road. You could even see the lane divider.

"Can you see anything? Any change in the display?"

"I can see that I'm on a big road, by eyesight and by the map!"

"I had a feeling. Okay, Llenn, thank you. Stay there and watch out. Listen up, everyone. This map will only show you the places you've seen for yourself. You'll only be able to see what's right in front of you while the mist is thick, so it's not going to tell you much for now."

Oh, I get it now! Llenn thought, mentally smacking her knee with recognition, since she was now lying down on the ground again.

It worked the same way that mapping did during regular play. For example, when you entered a new cave or underground city area, the system would automatically fill in the map area you had seen for yourself, but nothing else. Or in other words, "auto-mapping."

In tabletop RPGs and old-school games that only had 3D graphics, players would use graph paper to chart out the details manually, from what she heard. It seemed kind of fun, actually.

But she never expected to have to do mapping in Squad Jam. All the other events had shown her the entire map from the start of the game. The only exception was the cruise ship in SJ3, the secret final map.

"So," Clarence said, "does that mean it's better at the start to run around all over in the mist?"

"In terms of mapping, yes. But like we said earlier, it's really ineffective to wander around while the mist is thick, and more importantly, it increases the chances of running into an enemy," noted Miss Pitohui wisely. Clarence the student murmured with recognition, her question answered.

What happens once we meet up with teammates? Llenn wondered.

As if reading her mind, Pitohui went on, "And I'm guessing that the moment you meet up with a teammate, your map info will be combined. Out in the wilderness, you can always exchange map data with people coming from the other direction, right?"

Yes, I see, I see, Llenn thought.

"Hey, guys…if you think about it…we're just like gorillas…," said Fukaziroh, her voice ponderous with hidden meaning. "Get it? Because we're—"

"Gorillas in the mist, yeah," said Llenn, cutting her off. None of the others said a word, but for a while afterward, Clarence could be heard giggling to herself.

Llenn checked the watch she kept on the inside of her left wrist.

It was after 1:06. Less than four minutes until the first Satellite Scan.

In Squad Jam, the first ten minutes were generally more of a strategy time where you didn't go anywhere, but that time was coming to an end.

What should we do? Llenn wondered.

Once the Satellite Scan started, it would display the leader's position and team name. That would tell her the distance between herself and the other team leaders.

And based on the placement of the other dots, she would probably know where on the overall map she was.

In other words, if there were no dots to the west or south of her, she would know that she was in the southwest corner of the map.

But what to do after that point?

It would be possible to find SHINC's location and head in that direction. But there was no way she could do that without running into any other player as she went. On top of that, the compass didn't work for now, which meant that even though she'd know the leader's location, she would have to move bit by bit, drawing the map and correcting her direction.

Should they prioritize reuniting the team and have everyone come toward her?

No, that wouldn't work right away. None of them knew where *they* were yet.

They'd just have to move around until the map showed signs of change, and that would give them a good idea of where they were. Maybe they would slowly but surely come together, but it would raise the chances of enemy encounters along the way, and more importantly, it was likely that the hour would pass first.

It hurt that they wouldn't be able to use their comms, too. If they could just talk, there would be many different ways to get together, even if they started far away. And it would be much less lonely.

That stupid crappy writer just had to put together an obnoxious trial like this. If she ever ran across him, she'd put a bullet in his brain, or his ass, or both.

"I'm going to give each of you a plan to follow," said M, bypassing the team leader.

Llenn wasn't going to protest. If anything, M was more of a leader than she was.

I'm just a decoy leader, because I'm so tiny and cute and fast and small and adorable.

"Fuka."

"Yeah?"

"Just hide. If there's a freight car like in SJ3, that would be perfect. Once you've found a safe location, you don't need to move from there at all. Ignore the fighting. If you happen to spot someone, just slip past them, as long as it's not a teammate or SHINC. If you're lucky enough to meet one of us, you can offer support if you want, but there's no need to go anywhere if you're not safe."

"Had a feelin' you'd say exactly that. Gotcha! I'm good at playing hide-and-seek."

Uh-huh, agreed Llenn. Fukaziroh's grenade launchers could send devastating destruction to a distant (visible) enemy. Since there was no way to see into the distance now, it was pointless for her to try to fight.

She was only holding her pistol for show. She could fire thousands of shots without hitting anyone. Unless the gun misfired or something—maybe *then* it might actually hit someone by accident.

All that aside, it was best for Fukaziroh to stay still and hide. She could take a nice safe nap for the whole hour until the mist was gone.

"Shirley."

"Yeah."

"You were on snow? Take out your skis and zip around. When you spot a player, take them out in one shot and run. Just don't accidentally shoot an ally. All right?"

"I've already got them on. And yes, I will do that…but does Pitohui really count as an ally?" Shirley replied teasingly.

"Do whatever you like," M replied.

"Roger that," Shirley said. She *had* to be smirking to herself. Flashing those white teeth amid the fog, Llenn thought but did not say aloud.

"Clarence."

"Heigh-ho!"

"If you're on dry dirt, it's probably wasteland. You're going to have trouble hiding. Move as slowly as you can while the mist is thick. You can shoot any enemies you see, but get away from there as fast as you can. Once it's clear farther than the AR-57's firing range, try to get into a different biome and then hide."

"Okay! I'll just enjoy myself, then. It's not like I'm carrying anyone else's stuff. If I die, big whoop!"

"Lastly, Llenn."

So M didn't have any comments for Pitohui. Probably because he didn't need to give her advice. She was a demon, and she'd be fine on her own. If anything, any enemies around Pito should run for it now. They might still have a chance of survival. Or maybe not.

"Present!" Llenn replied, waiting for her orders. It was now 1:09:20.

"Switch to the Vorpal Bunnies until the mist starts to clear. The protective plate in your backup magazine pack will protect your back. Stay in place and watch the scan, and once the results disappear, just start running around, real fast. With your speed and size, you're not likely to get hit by anyone who actually sees you in the mist. If you can get in any sneak attacks, do it. If not, just run away. If you do attack, do it only once and then run. Don't turn back."

"Roger!"

Three seconds until the Satellite Scan. Llenn perfectly understood her orders.

She would use her speed and her Vorpal Bunnies and run around as fast as she could, watching out for obstacles. If she saw an enemy in the mist, she'd shoot them, if she could. But she didn't have to. Only if she could hit them, guaranteed. And then run away.

Until the mist cleared and she could use the effective range of her P90, which was about two hundred yards, she'd fight with her pistols.

M didn't specify this, but she was certain she should also be doing this for mapping purposes. The more information, the better.

"It's time. Best of luck, everyone. Just survive—and we'll meet up again later," M said, right as the clock hit 1:10:00.

The first Satellite Scan was beginning.

The Satellite Scan was explained as the work of a man-made satellite scanning the surface from space and sending the data down.

Based on the satellite's angle of inclination—the directions it came and went—the spot where the scan began was different every time. So was the speed with which the process happened and how soon it ended.

This one started from the north, going straight to the south, slowly lighting up little white dots. Llenn used the inward-pinch maneuver to zoom out as far as possible—meaning the entire map was (supposedly) visible.

She tapped the dots as soon as they appeared, checking the names they revealed.

Where's SHINC? Where's LPFM? Where on the map am I?

"Hrrg!" She issued a muffled yelp.

In the northwest part of the map—at least, based on the placement of the dots—she spotted the name MMTM.

And then to the east—making it the northeast corner—was the name SHINC.

"Guys!"

It was most definitely SHINC. Not some other tag that was confusingly similar.

If the four-corner theory held true, then she would be on the lower left corner, the southwest, or the lower right, the southeast.

"Please let it be the lower right, where I'm closer. Please, God of *Gun Gale*!" prayed Llenn, the only time she ever did such a thing. On the few occasions that Llenn actually prayed, it was to the God of *Gun Gale*, but she didn't know if it actually existed.

She did touch the dots that popped up near the center, but her heart wasn't in it. Some she recognized, some she did not.

When the scan finally got to the bottom, all the way to the south, she made another muffled yelp.

"Hrrg!"

There was no God of *Gun Gale*. She stopped believing. At least for now.

The dot labeled LPFM, indicating her location, was in the left-left corner, all the way to the southwest. The opposite corner from SHINC. As far away as she could possibly be.

"Ugh..."

She thought back on SJ2, the game on the day that she swore to kill Pitohui in order to save Elza's life. At the start of that game, too, they were on the diagonal corner, as distant as could be. She cursed the world then.

"Argh! Dammit! Fine, I'll do it!"

She chose to believe in herself, not in God.

As was the case in SJ2, she couldn't just sit in the corner and rot at the start. Squad Jam had just begun. She had a battle ahead of her that would probably last for two hours.

And being a battle, there was just one thing to do...

To believe in herself and fight.

Llenn placed the Satellite Scanner back in her shirt pocket and waved her left hand. She chose to alter her equipment and hit the ACCEPT button.

"See you later, P-chan."

The P90 resting on the concrete surface next to her vanished, as did the magazine pouches on either side of her waist.

"Let's go, Vor-chan."

They were replaced by a new accumulation of light that coalesced into two pink automatic pistols: the AM.45 Version Llenn, aka Vorpal Bunny.

Two black nylon holsters for the pistols appeared on her thighs, and a backpack holding plenty of backup ammunition hung over her shoulders. The white camo poncho automatically bulged outward to cover them.

She stood up, holding a Vorpal Bunny in each hand, and caught the rear sight on the right gun against the rear sight on the left, pulling the slide backward. Then she repeated it on the other side.

Cha-chik, cha-chik! Two satisfying metal clicks sounded in the mist, indicating that there was a .45 ACP bullet in each Vorpal Bunny's chamber.

Two pistol icons appeared in the bottom right corner of Llenn's vision, with the number *6* next to each, detailing the size of the magazine.

In her backpack she had another forty, giving her 240 bullets in total. There would be ammunition refills, too, so she should be able to shoot as much as she wanted, really.

"There we go!"

Llenn prepared to stand up, ready to go—and immediately heard a gunshot.

It was the sound of the firing itself and of a bullet creating a passing shock wave. After that, extremely clear through the mist, was a red bullet line.

"Eep!"

She flattened herself to the ground as bullet lines and their bullets passed over her head from right to left, like a broom being swept over her. They were high-pitched, high-speed shots, probably from a 5.56 mm rifle.

If she'd been even half a second quicker to stand, she would have been shot, that much was certain. If she was even of average player height, it would have hit her, too.

The fact that Llenn was tiny just barely saved her life.

She could see muzzle flashes lighting up through the thick mist. That was where the bullet lines were coming from.

Though she couldn't see them through the mist, a person was clearly there. They were ahead and on her left, about twenty to thirty yards away.

Dammit! Hey, you! You're as good as dead!

She took full advantage of her maxed-out agility to perform an ultra-high-speed forward crawl. This was a maneuver that only Llenn could perform.

Scuttling like the Insect-That-Shall-Not-Be-Named, she moved outside the enemy's visual range, she hoped. If they were right-handed, she would be moving toward their left.

During this time, the enemy fired in bursts, a few shots of automatic fire at a time in a repeated pattern. They weren't moving as they shot.

The shots kept coming endlessly.

Clearly, this player was using a magazine with an extreme number of bullets. Or maybe it was a machine gun with a belt-link feeder. Either way, it was bad news.

Though the enemy couldn't have seen Llenn at all, they must have heard the loud and proud click of her loading the Vorpal Bunnies. In other words, Llenn screwed up. She could easily have done it in a much quieter way.

When you make a mistake, you have to clean up your mess! she scolded herself, crawling forward like a soldier on fast-forward for about four seconds. Finally, she saw something in the mist that wasn't just road surface.

In the midst of the world of white, it looked like a fuzzy black stick at first, but eventually grew sharper, until it was clearly an enemy player.

An unfamiliar man wearing dark-green camouflage fatigues.

It wasn't a teammate or a member of SHINC—so it was someone she was allowed to kill.

He was using a 5.56 mm assault rifle, the M4A1. It had a hundred-round drum magazine like two barrels laid side by side. That was how he was firing so steadily for so long.

He was still firing in bursts, in fact, and the expression she could see on his face was clearly of fear. It was a rictus of terror, in fact.

Sure, it's scary. You're all alone in the mist, and then you hear the sound of a gun being loaded nearby, Llenn thought, carefully getting to her feet once she was completely behind her foe.

With a quick look around to see if there was anyone else sneaking up or sending a bullet line her way, Llenn concluded that she was good to go.

She slipped closer and pressed the Vorpal Bunnies upward against the back of his neck, just below the helmet. He had just finished shooting his hundred rounds, and the world was suddenly silent.

The touch of cold metal elicited a single sound from his throat that sounded surprisingly loud in the silence.

"Huh?"

The pair of gunshots sounded as one.

Llenn took off running.

All the shooting was sure to bring people over. She sprinted without hesitation, just as M instructed.

She didn't confirm the DEAD tag over the enemy she shot, but he'd taken two .45-caliber pistol bullets to the brain, so he couldn't be alive. He just couldn't.

Llenn ran, not knowing where she was going. She knew she was in the southwest corner of the vast map, but she didn't have a working compass to tell her the direction.

Ugh! Let the cards fall where they may!

There was no point to pondering a better plan if it got her killed. She decided to follow the center divider on the road beneath her boots. It was a flat, straight road.

If she ran up on the boundary of the map, then so be it. But then she could travel along that boundary. Once she'd done a certain amount of mapping, she'd be able to confirm her location and route on the second scan in eight minutes.

That was something only a team leader could do, and it was the best plan she could think of for now.

But I'm scared!

Running through such thick fog was basically like running with your eyes closed. Maybe it was slightly clearer than before, but she still couldn't see anything more than the ground in front of her feet for a few yards.

If there were any cars stopped in the road, she wouldn't be able to avoid them. She'd slam right into them, even if she hit the brakes.

But there was almost no way to die instantly from an impact. As long as you didn't do what she'd done during the playtest and try to kill yourself by slamming your head into a sturdy wall.

It's scary! But don't be scared! I'm the hardest to shoot when I'm running! It's the safest way to be!

Llenn did not stop. The thick soles of her combat boots pounded the concrete, producing only the smallest sound possible.

The next moment, about thirteen feet to her right, another black stick floated up, took the outline of a person, then passed by without a sound.

The encounter lasted all but an instant, but Llenn was able to summon the image crisply in her head.

It was a man wearing a Japanese Imperial Army uniform, perhaps an officer's coat.

He was one of the New Soldiers (NSS), a historical reenactment cosplay team that role-played as soldiers from the past who'd been sent to the future. He was carrying a Type 100 submachine gun, a historical relic.

Momentarily running across a person dressed from a different era in thick mist was kind of a ghostly experience. It was creepy. She felt like it was something out of an Akira Kurosawa film.

It wasn't clear if he had seen Llenn, too. She got the feeling he was pointing in a different direction. If he had spotted her, he might shoot at her—but after several seconds, she didn't hear any gunshots behind her. Maybe it was thanks to her camo poncho.

"I'm saved," she murmured, and continued on her way.

For better or for worse, the wide road went on and on. For now, there wasn't a single vehicle on the road.

Where was the road going? *Was* it going anywhere?

Llenn didn't have the answers, but that wasn't going to stop her. She glanced at her watch as she ran: one fifteen PM.

Then she looked ahead—thought she saw something dark—and slammed into it.

"Eek!"

"Eek!"

A pair of shrieks overlapped.

Llenn heard the shriek *as* she shrieked and, with all the momentum of her travel, rolled and tumbled down the road.

She knew only two things.

She had hit someone, lost her balance, and then slowed as she fell to the ground. And based on the voice, the other person was female.

Llenn was used to tumbling in *GGO*; like always, she drew her arms in, tucked her head and legs, and waited for her body to stop rolling.

After six and a half rotations, she came to a stop, skidding on her backpack.

"Hpp!"

She bounced like a spring, popping back up to her feet. That wasn't enough spinning to make *her* see birdies, no sir.

The person she ran into was already lost in the mist, without a trace of a silhouette.

What now? Llenn fretted.

She'd been in the process of looking up from her wristwatch, so all she'd been able to make out as they approached each other was a green lower half. She didn't get a good view of whomever she'd run into.

The scream made it clear it was a woman, but she had no idea if it was a teammate, or someone from SHINC, or someone else entirely.

It sounded kind of like a crisp, clear soprano voice, so it probably wasn't someone familiar like Fukaziroh, and it wasn't a lower-pitched voice like Pitohui's or Boss's—but there was no guarantee it wasn't Shirley, Clarence, or one of the other SHINC girls.

What should I do? What's the right answer?

If it was a friend, she should say something. If it was a foe, she should shoot or run.

If it was a friend, they would say something. If it was a foe, they would shoot.

What should I do, what should I do, what should I—?

Within a fraction of a second of indecision, she heard the voice speak through the mist.

"Hey, Llenn."

Ah!

Once again, she was required to make a split-second judgment. Her head spun even harder than before.

The other girl knew who she was.

Well, if she'd seen her when they collided, she could have easily recognized Llenn based on her being the tiniest player in Squad Jam and with pink boots and fatigues peeking out from under the poncho.

And just to be clear, there was only one tiny shrimp wearing all pink in Squad Jam. There could only be one.

Also, the voice did not sound familiar. It didn't seem to be a teammate or member of SHINC. It was much more likely this was someone else.

However, it *was* a voice she had heard before on multiple occasions. And recently.

Who is it? And what should I do?

To run, to fight, or to speak—that is the question, Llenn Hamletted. It was a three-choice question.

She could probably get away if she ran. The mist was just as thick for both of them.

But in *GGO*, especially in Squad Jam, you ought to eliminate your enemies.

She ought to charge and fire her Vorpal Bunnies into the mist in the direction of the voice.

But no, that would just get her shot. And if the other girl had a rifle, Llenn would lose. Maybe she could shoot once, taking the enemy by surprise, and utilize a scuttling-insect maneuver to swing around behind her and *boom!*

Llenn did neither of these things.

"What's up?" she replied.

The other person had spoken to her, and she recognized the voice. These facts alone demanded a response. But she didn't forget to flop to the ground as she did so.

"I'm heading over there. If you shoot, I'll shoot, too."

"I'm not going to shoot! As long as you don't!"

"Good idea. I don't want a mutual KO right at the start."

So they both had the same idea.

In order to identify the other person, they'd need to be just a few yards apart in the mist. If they launched into a full attack at that distance, there was a very high chance that both would die and be out of Squad Jam.

Even still, Llenn waited with the Vorpal Bunnies in her hands. She was lying down, her arms pointed forward, elbows slightly bent, with the guns held at a slight inward angle.

But she didn't put her fingers on the triggers. Producing bullet lines would be an indication to the other girl that she intended to shoot.

Eventually, a dark figure appeared out of the white mist, her details becoming clearer, like a video of something melting, played in reverse.

It was a beautiful woman who looked to be about twenty years old.

She had pale skin, short red hair, and a beanie on top. Resting over her cheekbones was a pair of smartglasses that would display information before your eyes, in the style of fashionable sports shades.

She wore tiger-stripe camo pants, with a simple black hoodie and a tactical chest rig, also in tiger-stripe pattern.

Around her neck and shoulders hung an RPD, a Soviet light machine gun, with a shortened barrel and a drum magazine attached. Holstered on her right hip was an American military issue 9 mm automatic handgun, the M17.

"Oh..."

Llenn knew who it was. Belatedly, she realized that *that's* whose voice she'd been hearing.

Her name was Vivi.

The sole woman on ZEMAL, who joined them before SJ4.

She'd known Fukaziroh back in *ALO*—they were on opposing fairy races, so they'd been enemies.

In SJ4, she led ZEMAL to push LPFM to the brink, nearly wiping them out. But on Pitohui's suggestion, she let them go, for the sake of the bet with Fire.

During the recent Five Ordeals quest, they temporarily worked together to defeat Mecha-Dragon, and they even spoke a little at the pub afterward. She'd killed the dog and didn't get the true ending, and had waited for them to show up.

The fact that she was here now proved she wasn't ZEMAL's leader. That wasn't a surprise, however. She'd led an excellent roving squad in SJ4, too.

"Good day to you, Llenn."

When she saw that Vivi's RPD wasn't pointed at her, Llenn lowered her Vorpal Bunnies.

She could just open fire on her, and in some sense, maybe she should. Vivi was a brilliant leader and adviser, someone who had taken ZEMAL from laughingstock all the way to champions in SJ4.

Killing her right now might've been Llenn's best and only chance to execute an action that would be necessary to win SJ5.

"Hello..."

But Llenn did not shoot her.

She must have had a reason for saying hello. Llenn wanted to know what it was and if she could make use of it.

Vivi approached to within six feet and crouched. Llenn lifted herself up off the ground and into a hunched-over position. It would be easier to run this way than on her hands and feet.

They hadn't produced any gunshots here, so no other enemies who may be in the area should have noticed them, but vigilance was still key.

Vivi was crouched on Llenn's left up ahead. She wasn't facing Llenn directly. Then she pointed at her own eyes with index and middle fingers, and pointed ahead of her.

Aha. She wants us to watch each other's back, Llenn understood. She nodded broadly enough to be noticeable through her large poncho hood and did as directed. She kept her eyes peeled for signs of movement, with Vivi's pretty face framed on her left.

Vivi went into her inventory, then waved her arm to send the window to Llenn. They were just close enough to be able to trade items directly.

The little black window was visible only to Llenn. It said: *Connect comm? Y/N*

Interesting. This would allow them to communicate with a minimum of vocalization. She hit *Y* without thinking twice and heard Vivi's voice loud and clear in her left ear, despite it being only a soft murmur.

"Crazy rules, huh? That sponsor is a real handful, isn't he?"

"Seriously."

"I have a goal in mind. I want my team to have their fun shooting, and then I can guide them to victory."

"I see. Sounds tough," Llenn replied casually.

But they might actually do it, she thought, her heart pounding. *Should I actually go ahead and kill Vivi…? Or would murdering her now after our little truce leave a bad aftertaste? Still, my teammates will probably say, 'Good job'…especially Pitohui. Fukaziroh would definitely prioritize winning the game over being a good person, so she'd probably do it. But even still, I just don't— Arrrrgh…*

Llenn's mind wandered back and forth, bouncing between options like an indecisive young teen.

"So do you want to team up until two o'clock?" Vivi suggested.

It was 1:17.

"Uh-huh… Well, two's better than one in this situation, and a team's better than two. The more eyes, the better off we'll be. But..."

Llenn checked her watch while remaining focused on the surroundings. She understood exactly what Vivi was thinking. This was precisely what you needed to survive the first hour of SJ5.

But there was something Llenn needed to confirm. She didn't have the time to feel out what the other girl was plotting. She'd just have to ask directly.

"For reasons I'm not sure of, I have a bounty of a hundred million credits on my head. Where's my guarantee that you won't shoot me in the back of the head at exactly two o'clock?"

"There isn't one. Just as there's no guarantee you won't shoot me at one fifty-nine," Vivi replied, which was a more likable answer than playing coy.

"Got it. One more question. We have an agreement to meet up with our friends in SHINC and fight alongside them. The special rules make that impossible for now, but they're basically teammates, and I'm trying to go northeast to find them. Assuming I can tell the direction."

"Sure thing. I'll treat them as allies, just like our own teammates. Until two o'clock. But..."

"But what?"

"If our teammates located elsewhere are shooting one another without knowing about us, there's no blaming each other."

"...Got it. No hard feelings."

With all of that cleared up, Llenn asked Vivi a simple logistical question. "ZEMAL's leader was in the bottom right of the map, the southeast, right? Are you sure you don't need to head that way?"

"I'm all right. I gave the others their orders ahead of time. Nobody move, except for the leader. Stay hidden for the entire hour. And to the leader, I said, 'Good luck!'"

"I see."

Just like Fukaziroh. A team with immense firepower needed to restrain itself within heavy mist. Hiding was the best option.

Except for whoever was the leader and had their location given away on the map. Good luck to them.

"So I can spend some time helping you find your friends, if you want. If we can thin out the numbers of enemies in the meantime, even better," Vivi said.

Llenn checked her wristwatch. It was 1:19. Sixty seconds until the scan.

There was no time to make up her mind.

"Agreed on all counts. Let's go with that. It'll be nice working with you," Llenn replied.

Vivi's pretty face wore a mature smile. "Same to you, Llenn."

"Just one more question I've always wanted to ask."

"What is it?"

"What kind of relationship did you have with my friend Fukaziroh in the world of fairies?"

It was 1:19:50 now.

"It would take all night to explain that to you," Vivi said.

"Let's watch the scan, then."

"Agreed."

SECT.4

CHAPTER 4

A Battle for Two

CHAPTER 4
A Battle for Two

The second Satellite Scan of SJ5 started from the south at 1:20.

Llenn returned her left Vorpal Bunny to its holster and stared at the screen of her scanner in a crouch.

She knew where she was. She'd traveled about two-thirds of a mile north from the start. She thought she'd run quite a ways, but it wasn't that much. Hardly any ground at all, really. Her time had been taken up by other things.

But she did know a bit more about the map.

The road she'd been running on was displayed now. According to the image, it was indeed a freeway: six lanes in each direction, going directly north and south.

It was only a tiny little slice within the white, but it was better than not being able to see anything. Part of her even felt a new kind of excitement about it. *I'll run all over the map to paint in the white canvas!* she thought positively. Assuming she didn't die first.

"Huh?"

But upon closer inspection, there was more freeway displayed north of her dot on the map, where she hadn't traveled yet.

It was Vivi who figured it out before Llenn did. With her scanner in her left hand, she said, "I can see your northward travels on my map, too. I came south from where I started. It looks like being within item-trading range will automatically combine your map data, whether friend or foe."

"I see."

So you didn't need to be teammates for it to work. Maybe it would even work with a corpse? That was valuable information to learn. *Should I shoot Vivi now? No, I can wait a bit longer.*

She watched the scan move farther north, but not much changed.

No teams had vanished yet. That made sense. Even if a team leader had the luck of being shot in a spontaneous battle, the designation would simply travel to the next person in line. Since all six members would be scattered around the map, it would take some colossally bad collective luck for all of them to die this quickly.

Finally, the screen showed Llenn what she wanted to know most.

SHINC's leader, Boss, had thankfully moved southwest. She was coming closer to Llenn.

"Good…"

So that made their next course of action…

"We travel northeast, watching out for enemies. Let's step off the highway."

She didn't need to explain anything to Vivi. That made things easy.

"May I leave you in the lead, Llenn? I'll follow about a hundred feet behind you, with my map up and zoomed in. If our direction starts drifting, I'll let you know."

Aha. So even in the mist and without a compass, they could travel northeast. The freeway already displayed on the map would be the needle indicating north and south. So as long as they charted a course forty-five degrees to the right, away from the line, they were going the correct way.

"But aren't you afraid you'll lose sight of me, Vivi?"

Even though visibility was slowly growing and they could hear each other talk, would a hundred feet make it too difficult?

"Not at all. We'll use this."

Vivi removed a round, flat item about three-quarters of an inch wide and half as thick from her inventory. It was colored black and had a little plastic dome cover on top, another half an inch tall.

Although she'd never seen this item before, Llenn knew what it was: an LED light. It would light up or blink, so you could use it to indicate your location, paths you'd taken, or rooms you'd already cleared out.

In most cases, you'd use it on the strobe setting, a blinking function for maximum visibility. You could also adjust the blink interval, the total illumination time before shutoff, the number of blinks, and the strength of the light. In short, it was a tiny lighthouse.

"So you want me to go in front, shining like a spotlight?"

A powerful light source like this would probably cut through most of the mist, the same way the muzzle flash did for the guy she killed earlier. But that would also draw the attention of the enemies who might be—no, definitely were—nearby. It would get you shot and done for.

"You're half correct. This is set to infrared mode. It's invisible to the naked eye," Vivi said, bowing her head as though in thanks. That motion revealed another one of the same item, attached to the back of her beanie.

It was placed so casually that it just looked like a design accent on her cap. It didn't look like it was producing any light at all.

"It shows up on the smartglasses that I and the rest of my team wear. It's not anywhere near regular visibility, but you can see it at about a hundred yards in this mist. I set my beanie down earlier to test it."

"Interesting..."

By rule, there were no sight-enhancing items or special skills that could allow you to see more terrain or characters in this event.

But light itself, whether visible or infrared, was apparently removed from this rule. It was part of the setup. Apparently, having visible light work but infrared invalid wouldn't be fair to the people who chose to bring those items.

"As long as you have it on your head, I'll be able to follow."

Vivi tossed the item to Llenn, who caught it. She placed it on the back of the hood of her snow camo poncho, and it stayed stable, as if connected by magnets. How convenient.

"Well, I'll borrow this, then...but I won't be able to tell if any members of ZEMAL are around."

What, don't you have a backup pair of your fancy-schmancy glasses? she could imagine Fukaziroh saying. But Llenn was more genteel than that, and made the same point delicately and indirectly. Hopefully the message got across.

"Unfortunately, I don't have backup smartglasses. So I'll give orders from the rear, instead."

So she did get the hint. Llenn couldn't tell if that was because she really didn't have an extra pair, or if Vivi was lying about it.

"So if you tell me not to shoot whoever's coming, it's ZEMAL. But anyone else, it's up to my judgment what to do? Since it might be my own ally..."

"Exactly. It sounds like a plan to me," Vivi said.

But it's a lot more work for me! Llenn realized. *This team-up isn't exactly on even footing. She has me as the vanguard, right on her reins...*

She couldn't just turn around and go back on their agreement, though, and even in this situation, she had a better chance of survival than going alone.

"All right. Let's go," she said, without much choice in the matter. This was just wasting time.

Vivi's scary. Watch out for her, Llenn thought but did not say aloud.

Instead, she recalled a conversation she had with Miyu about a month earlier.

⁂ ⁂ ⁂

Saturday, August 29th.

"Hey, Miyu...what's that Vivi girl like?"

SJ4 was three days ago, and today had been the Dumped by Fire Nishiyamada—Consoling Karen Kohiruimaki Karaoke Festival (with Special Guest Elza Kanzaki) Event, which was now over.

Miyu had flown in from Hokkaido without hotel considerations just to spy on Karen's first-ever date, so she wound up spending the night at Karen's apartment.

She was sitting cross-legged on the living room rug, eating her third serving of ice cream, totally nude from the bath except for one of Karen's T-shirts, when Karen asked her the question.

Vivi was an excellent player, a mastermind who had just led ZEMAL to a perfect victory in SJ4.

Based on their conversations in-game, she had been a salamander, the fire fairies from *ALO*, whose territory bordered that of Fukaziroh's sylphs, and due to their constant run-ins, she had destroyed Fukaziroh on numerous occasions in a rather one-sided manner.

Miyu placed the three empty ice cream cups on the table, spreading them out evenly. Lastly, she gave the flat plastic spoon one final lick before tossing it into an empty cup.

Her gaze traveled off into the distance. "Her...? Oh, I know her," she said, her words pure poetry.

"Yeah, I know that you know her."

"It's a long story. And a very old one..."

"You're exaggerating."

"Did you know there are three kinds of aces?"

"What are you talking about?"

Miyu pointed at the empty ice cream cups one at a time. "Those who seek strength...those who live for pride...and those who can read the tide of battle. Those are the three types."

"Uh-huh..."

"And she is..."

"Which one?"

"...all three."

"Uh-huh...," Karen repeated, listening intently to Miyu's hard-boiled speech.

Incidentally, the whole speech about different kinds of aces was ripped directly from a rival character in a certain famous flight combat game, but Karen had no idea, so she didn't react to it. How could she know?

Miyu ignored the fact that her reference was ignored. "To be honest, she's a hell of a player. She's incredible. If you had to break down what makes her so incredible..."

She was finally getting to the answer. It had taken a long time to get here.

"...it's that she's good at using people."

"Ah, I see... That's why she managed to manipulate—er, that sounds bad—lead the Machine-Gun Lovers and make the most of their strengths."

"Exactly. She's really tough solo, too, though. Not only are her stats excellent, she's used to full-diving, so her movements are smooth. Real good flier, to boot. From what I've heard, she just travels from VR game to VR game. She's spent a looong time on the other side. The name Vivi holds sway in many games. And the source of her name is a mystery. I've asked her many times, but she won't tell me."

"Uh-huh."

"Now, Vivi as a salamander looked totally different. She was a big, buff warrior lady. But she was famous as a party strategist among the salamanders. They would say, 'If she's in command, you'll never lose.' She understood not just her allies' weapons and fighting styles, but also their personalities, and she'd give them accurate orders to get just the right results out of them."

"Uh-huh."

"She knows a lot, too. One day, there was an aerial battle between a party of sylphs and a party of salamanders—as you know, you can fly in *ALO*. It's harder to use combination tactics in the air than it is on the ground, so normally it just devolves into hectic one-on-one dogfights. But in this particular fight, the sylphs got wiped out. They all got turned into fires in the sky without knocking out a single foe."

"Fires?"

"Yeah. If you die in *ALO*, you stay in place as a fire called a Remain Light for one minute, and you can see what's happening. You know what happens after you die. In our neck of the woods, you'd call dying 'turning into fire,' you see. No idea if that's common throughout *ALO*."

"Ohhh."

"Just keep that in mind for when you visit *ALO*."

"I'll remember it. Not that I'm ever going there."

"Anyhoo, the sylph team got beat big-time, and when they discussed their defeat afterward, someone said, 'The way they fought was similar to how the Germans fought aerial battles in WWII.' What that means is, every plane has another one behind it, sticking close, to prevent anyone from getting on their rear. And there's two groups of them—so four in total. That basically eliminates blind spots and makes it impossible to sneak up on them from behind. What was it called again…? It's like Schbababa, or Schururu, or something like that. Sounds Germanish, right?"

Ignoring that last question, Karen murmured, "Interesting."

"So according to that military weirdo, *ALO* flight makes people move more like propeller planes from WWII rather than modern jets. So we concluded that she must have played a bunch of those aerial combat games. Eventually, we came to a bold conclusion: Don't fight any formation including Vivi in the air. Fight on the ground."

"How is that bold?"

"It's good strategy to avoid a losing battle. Basically, just watch out for her."

"I see. So Vivi's the real deal, and her leadership bringing the best out of that team was legit. I gotcha. I'll watch out for her," Karen agreed, and finished off her barley tea.

Miyu watched her intently. "By the way, Karen."

"What?"

"I must go to the bathroom! Don't look for me! I won't be back for a while!"

"That's what you get for eating so much ice cream!"

* * *

Twenty-one minutes after the start of SJ5, Llenn was walking through the mist.

The thick layer was supposed to be clear after an hour, but it didn't feel like it had lightened very much. The pace of its clearing was much slower than she anticipated. At this rate, it didn't feel like their visibility was going to be perfectly clear by two o'clock.

So either the process would speed up as time went on or the mist would stay thick until it abruptly vanished right at the hour. Knowing the lump of human garbage who designed the rules, it would more than likely be the latter.

Very soon after walking off the highway at an angle, Llenn hit the soggy earth of the median strip. The highway was eight lanes in each direction, so the median was probably pretty spacious, too. Once she crossed it, there would likely be another eight lanes of highway going the opposite direction.

In other words, the highway was likely over two hundred yards wide in total. It was like a great river. Since it was based on American freeways, it wasn't elevated like Japanese expressways, but straight along the ground.

Battling the fear of unseen enemies, Llenn clutched her Vorpal Bunnies and walked. Though she couldn't see her through the mist, Vivi was supposedly following about a hundred feet behind. Through the comm, Llenn told her erstwhile teammate, "The median's over. I'm heading back over the lanes going the other way."

"I'm following. Your angle is good. Start crossing the road just the way you're going."

So according to Vivi, who was watching the map being filled in, she was heading northeast the way they wanted.

"Got it."

Llenn stayed low, mindful of her surroundings.

Her boots hit concrete again. The pace was that of a brisk walk. She was watching the space ahead and to the sides. If any dark shadows appeared, it was a player. She'd have to identify friend or foe and react accordingly.

It was a difficult situation, one that kept her nerves taut for a lengthy period of time. But she couldn't whine about it.

Llenn crossed the third lane of eight—she was almost in the center.

And that was when it appeared.

From behind on her right—outside her field of view—she heard a low engine rumble. It rapidly got much louder.

"Huh?"

By the time Llenn had turned around to see, a dark, ferocious beast was coming out of the mist.

It was a black mass, six and a half feet wide and five and a half feet tall, roaring toward her location. A fraction of a second later, she realized it was an automobile.

"Eep!"

She didn't know the exact model, but she could tell it was a low-riding station wagon.

It slid out of the mist and raced right for Llenn. She couldn't see the driver because of the reflection on the windshield, but they probably weren't explicitly trying to run her over.

Presumably, they found those wheels on the highway and were trying to make use of them to cross as much distance as possible. But they were driving through heavy mist, so if anyone suddenly popped in, well, taking them out, too, just made sense. And with Llenn still in her white poncho, the driver might not even have seen her.

Llenn could see everything as time slowed with intense concentration. The car was just a few yards away now.

She had a Vorpal Bunny in each hand, but even if she managed to hit the driver through the windshield, that wouldn't stop the car. Nothing would, at this point.

There was no time to dodge to the right or left. The tires were wide, and as a station wagon, it was fairly tall. But this wasn't like the Humvee in SJ2; she wouldn't be able to hit the ground and let it pass over her. She had the big backpack on anyway.

Oh, I'm dead.

She mentally prepared herself to be sent sailing into the horizon like a home-run ball.

But as she did so, she thought, *No, I won't die! I refuse to die this early!*

It was the last little bit of resistance she could muster. If she couldn't go below or to the sides, it left only above.

"Taaa!"

She used all the leg strength she had to perform a powerful jump.

In her view, the car sank as it raced closer; in reality, she was jumping upward as the car passed below her.

Please don't hit my feet! she prayed, folding them in as best she could.

And then the black beast roared past, just below her. She felt a new wind lifting her, sending the back of the poncho flipping upward.

As she reached the peak of her jump and began to descend, she twisted to her left and saw the dark shape vanish into the thick mist behind her. It was already out of sight when her feet hit the ground. The engine roar was growing quieter.

* * *

That was a close one, she thought, relieved. But it was too early for that.

Without any time to rest, she heard the fierce squeal of tires braking. It sounded like someone screaming.

Apparently, the antilock braking system was broken on the vehicle's tires. It was totally run-down, so that wasn't surprising.

Every player in *GGO* had the Ignore skill active against jokes about how a ruined post-apocalyptic world could possibly feature abandoned vehicles with working engines *and* adequate tire pressure.

"What's happening?" asked Vivi calmly, right as Llenn landed.

"I almost got run over by a car! I jumped over it, but it's stopping!" she shouted. She didn't know *why* the car had stopped, though.

"They must have seen the pink of your legs, Miss Wanted Woman."

Now it made sense. Too much sense.

"Ugh! Dammit!"

It was that reward. The driver must have realized it was Llenn by the flash of pink on her legs. No wonder they hit the brakes.

Meeting up with your teammates? That could wait. There was a major payout on the line. With that much cash, you could live in luxury for six months, the driver might have thought, not that Llenn could know that.

"They'll turn around right away and try to run you over."

"Ugh!"

"Do you have any grenades?"

"No!"

In SJ1, Llenn carried two plasma grenades. Since SJ2, she'd either taken some or not, after weighing the benefits against the danger of a chain reaction if one got hit by a bullet.

This time she'd left them behind to allow for the extra weight of the Vorpal Bunnies. If she had one, she might have been able to drop it right in front of her, but it was too late for that now.

"Shoot your pistols and retreat to the south as fast as you can."

"And what will happen?"

"Just do it."

She felt like Vivi was manipulating her again, but decided to go ahead and do it anyway. If Fukaziroh admitted Vivi was good at this, she had to have a plan. Probably. Most likely. And if she didn't, there'd be hell to pay.

"Got it!"

Oh, whatever! Llenn thought. She confirmed the safeties were off on the Vorpal Bunnies and squeezed them harder.

In the Five Ordeals, she had accidentally activated the safety from squeezing too hard, which saved her life, but that was just pure dumb luck.

A beast roared from the north, where the car had gone. It was revving the engine. No stopping it from rushing back toward her again.

Llenn transitioned from back-stepping to a run. It was a full sprint going backward. This was slower than running forward, obviously, but Llenn was fast in every regard, so it was still a speedy pace. It looked almost comical, like video being rewound. But…

No matter how fast I am, I can't outrun a car…

There was no way to beat the beast that came looming out of the mist.

Llenn didn't know what Vivi's plan was, but she started firing the Vorpal Bunnies anyway. She sprayed bullets, alternating right and left, as she backed away.

She wasn't a great shot with a pistol, but with a target this big, she was presumably hitting her mark. There were visible sparks coming up, at least.

That wasn't going to be enough to take down this beast, however. The driver could tell from the bullet lines that they were being shot at. They were probably leaning forward in the seat to make a smaller target.

It was hard to imagine that a couple of .45-caliber pistol rounds were going to stop the car's engine. And even if she was lucky enough to hit one, a popped tire or two wouldn't stop the current momentum.

The car's face finally came clear through the mist, which billowed around it as it charged.

There was a spiderweb crack on the windshield, but the driver's hands were clearly visible. Still no idea who it was.

She also realized there were assault rifle muzzles pointing out of both of the rear side windows. The guns started blazing.

They weren't shooting in the direction the car was driving, but opened at an angle, fully automatic. This way, if Llenn tried to escape to the sides, she'd run across their lines of fire.

Uh-oh, I'm screwed. I'll have to go up again…but I just barely made it last time. Can I do it right again while I'm running backward…?

She was feeling a bit of self-doubt when the car was shrouded in gunfire and sparks.

It was the right side of the car—left from Llenn's perspective—that caught the bullets and produced the sparks. Glass shattered.

A shower of light came from off to the left, lighting up the side of the car with tracer rounds and bullet lines. The side doors on the right lit up with the display.

It lasted for one, two, then three seconds. At last, the car shook, and the gunfire from the rear seat stopped.

The car made an abrupt turn toward Llenn's right as she retreated, its rear tires squealing. Eventually, it vanished into the mist again, totally out of sight.

Then a massive sound emerged that had nothing to do with gunshots.

It was a complex combination of destruction that sounded like *boomkuttacrakkabwash!*

Most likely, the car had flipped over. It was a traffic accident.

Llenn stopped running and heard Vivi ask, "Are you okay?"

"I'm fine. Was that you, Vivi?"

"Yes. Thanks for playing the bait. I could see the bullet lines and the sparks, which made it easy to aim at the car."

"I see..."

Vivi had run over through the mist and shot at the car, saving Llenn.

Her primary weapon was a light machine gun called the RPD.

"Light" referred only to the total weight, with the operative phrase being "for a machine gun." When you included the ammo, it was a good twenty pounds, over twice the weight of your average assault rifle.

It fired Soviet 7.62 × 39 mm rounds, the same as the AK-47 series. They would pass right through a typical car door like it was paper.

Getting ten of those per second on your side would be devastating. The RPD's drum magazine had a hundred rounds in it, connected by belt links. She'd fired for about three seconds, so the driver and the two passengers must have taken several shots each.

"I doubt they're still alive, but can you check for me?"

Once again, it was a dangerous task, but Llenn owed the girl for saving her life.

"Got it."

She crept through the mist in the direction of the crashing sound with her Vorpal Bunnies at the ready.

It took no time at all to find them. The car had flipped over onto its roof right where the highway met the shoulder. The tires were pointing toward the sky.

Llenn didn't know the model. She just knew it was a car, the end.

If M were present, however, he would have been able to tell her that it was a Subaru Outback Wilderness, a large station wagon built for off-road conditions.

The Outback had lost all of its windows, its right side was pocked with bullet holes, and its top was all dented in; it was in a miserable state. In addition, one of the tires had blown clean off. The designer of the car would be crying if they could see it now.

Llenn was able to identify the state of the three riders immediately. She didn't need to crouch and look inside—it was simply obvious. The DEAD tags were bright and visible outside the vehicle, even through the mist.

The players had been tossed out of the car during its tremendous rolling act and were now lying in the street. Real world or virtual, this is what happens if you don't wear your seat belt.

"Confirming: All of them are dead," Llenn said, eyeing their clothes, "and none of them are with us."

That was a relief. Of course, it was obvious from the point of the second ramming charge that they were neither Llenn's teammates nor SHINC nor ZEMAL, from the way Vivi shot at them. Still, it never hurt to check.

The three players, all men, were covered in red damage effects. One wore reddish-brown camo. He was a member of the team that came together under the dome in SJ2.

Another wore American military tiger-stripe camo and had assembled an outfit that looked like Vietnam War garb. He was in NSS.

The last of the three wore a sci-fi-like bodysuit with protectors on his joints. She'd never seen him in any videos.

This variation made it obvious that the three were not from the same team, but had joined together under the misty circumstances for survival, just like Llenn and Vivi had. That strategy knocked them right out of SJ5 together, too.

Llenn was about to stand up and leave when Vivi said into her ear, "Is anyone carrying a grenade on their person?"

She stared at the bodies. The man in the tiger-stripe camo had machine-gun pouches on either side, along with a couple of M26A1 grenades, which the United States used in Vietnam. His cosplay dedication was impressive; even his weapons matched the era.

"Yes."

"Can you stick as many of them under the body as you can, then pull the pin on one?"

"...Ah, I see."

Llenn quickly did as she said. She could tell what Vivi was planning.

After about ten minutes, these bodies would vanish from the game. At that point, the grenades Llenn touched would be treated as plunder, so they would remain on the map.

When that happened, the lever that had been held down by the weight of the dead body would come free without the safety pin in place, and it would explode in three or four seconds.

It was very unlikely this would just so happen to damage anyone, but a series of consecutive grenade explosions in the mist would certainly do a lot to alarm anyone nearby.

What a nasty idea to have, Llenn thought, both impressed and disgusted. She got right to work; grenade traps were a familiar tactic for her. She'd done them a lot in the past, particularly when startling her PK targets. *I was kinda messed-up back then. I mean, really messed-up.*

The task was finished nice and quick, and Llenn dashed away from the area. *Someone* had surely heard the fierce sounds of battle. They would either come rushing over to take advantage or run the other way because they didn't want to die in the mist.

I hope it's the latter, Llenn prayed, squeezing her Vorpal Bunnies.

After several seconds of walking, listening carefully for the sound of anyone attacking, she heard Vivi conclude, "Doesn't seem like there's another group of them." And she enjoyed a brief moment of relief.

Then she cautiously crossed the highway and said to Vivi, "May I ask you a question?" It was really weighing on her mind.

"What is it?"

"Why were you so well prepared? Most people would never expect to use an infrared strobe light," she asked boldly.

Because of the time of day that the event was held, night combat was next to impossible in Squad Jam, so why would you expect to need an infrared light? Maybe for a cave or some other sealed indoor space, but creating a truly dark area would basically make it impossible for any players who didn't have nighttime gear. You would assume that any environment they'd put into the map would be dark, but not so dark that you couldn't see.

Particularly because in Squad Jam, you had to leave behind anything you didn't absolutely need. Every gram of unnecessary weight removed was a gram that could be taken up by something useful instead.

"Oh?" Vivi said, taken by surprise. Her surprise took Llenn by surprise.

"What do you mean, 'Oh'?"

"You were the ones who taught us during the Five Ordeals. That sponsor loves to re-create in-game versions of the situations in his novels."

Yes, that had happened.

"So...you read them? *All* of them?"

"Yes. And there was one short story where the protagonist ran away from home and was stuck in thick mist, and they started talking to their bicycle, and eventually the bicycle started talking back, but in the end, you find out it was all just the protagonist hallucinating. The story was called 'Misty's Journey.'"

I didn't know about that, because I never read it... Also, that title's not actually that dumb...for once, Llenn thought.

"So I brought the lights along, just in case there was a battle in thick mist."

"Interesting... Very, very interesting..."

Though it was pointless to regret it now, if she'd actually read all those autographed books she won from winning SJ1, they might have come in very handy for her. Well, too late now.

At the same time, Llenn could only grapple privately with another question.

Who is *this Vivi chick?*

•

Once past the highway to the northeast, they found themselves in a residential area.

After they left the paved road, there was empty ground for about a hundred feet, which turned into flat residential lots. There were no fences between them.

Because of the mist, it was hard to tell how far the houses went, however.

They were arranged American style—mansions spread apart with spacious yards and garages along the street. To a Japanese audience, they might look like mansions, but to an American audience, maybe they were perfectly average homes.

Regardless, garages with several big cars in them, expansive yards, and private pools were *not* normal for Japan.

Since there was so much space, they didn't need to build two stories. Nearly all of them were one-floor homes.

The ground between the homes and the street, which would have once contained lawns, were now dried dirt. There was no grass.

The exteriors of the buildings were in tatters. Roofs and walls made of wood were rotting away. Glass windows and doors were sometimes intact, sometimes broken. Some homes were half-collapsed, and some had completely given way.

Of course, in a setting like *GGO*, it would be unnatural for there to be any brand-spanking-new buildings. If so, they were a trap. You wouldn't want to go near those.

Since there were now structures in sight, it was easier to gauge the visibility through the mist than before. At this point, details were crisp and clear up to about twenty yards. They quickly got fuzzy after that, but you could see if there was a dark shadow at around thirty or forty yards, which told you that a house was there.

Llenn proceeded down a nice flat road surface, which coincidentally happened to be heading northeast. She kept her head low.

This was because the roads were wide and the houses spread apart, so even if someone was lurking in wait inside one of the houses, she might be far enough away that they couldn't see her yet.

With each step, she listened carefully, but there wasn't a sound.

Walking down the silent street with houses floating eerily past her made them seem even more desolate than usual. It was like being in a horror movie.

This is scary. Oooh, it's scary. Also, it's scary.

If Vivi hadn't been around to hear it, she might have whined once or twice, or ten times, just to work out her nerves a little bit.

Briefly, she wondered if she should switch from the Vorpal Bunnies back to the P90, but decided to stick with what she had for now. The P90 had better firepower, but the defensive shields in her backpack could block shots from behind her and possibly save her life.

After what felt like a very long time but was barely a minute in actuality, Llenn reached a T-intersection in the suburbs, fortunately without getting shot at.

The road split to both sides at ninety-degree angles. On the left corner was a single transport truck, rusted and dilapidated.

Before her was the dark shadow of an especially large house, which loomed menacingly overhead, blocking their path.

Llenn asked Vivi, "The road splits left and right up here. Which way should we go? Or should I just keep heading straight and walk around the big house in front of me?"

It would throw off their angle, but if she stayed on the road, the IR strobe light and smartglasses would make it easier for Vivi to track her location. It would also just be easier to walk down.

Straight ahead was a shortcut to SHINC, but going inside the house or around it would mean passing through impediments that might cause Vivi to lose sight of her.

Llenn waited for her answer.

Whatever Vivi the wise strategist says, I'll follow faithfully. Yes, that would be best. Obviously the right answer.

She waited a few more seconds but heard nothing.

"Vivi?"

No response.

"Vivi?"

No response.

Shiver...

Shiver, shiver...

A virtual chill ran down Llenn's spine.

Wait, did I...get left behind? she thought. But upon closer consideration, there was nothing Vivi stood to gain by doing that.

For one thing, she'd left the LED with Llenn. If she didn't get that back, her ZEMAL teammates would likely wind up very confused down the line.

That left only one possibility.

She was in a situation that did not allow her to talk.

And the only situation that could cause that was an enemy in very close proximity.

Shiver, shiver.

Llenn moved away from the spot immediately. She once again traveled like a certain unspeakable insect and hid behind the rusted-out truck on the left side of the intersection.

Maybe Vivi couldn't speak, but the sound from the comm was audible only inside the ear of the wearer. Even still, Llenn spoke into it as quietly as she could.

"I'm hidden."

Then she heard a loud voice say, "Goddammit! I can't do this anymore!"

Eep! She nearly shrieked.

The voice belonged to a man, and it was very close by. She heard him speaking aloud from just down the road she'd traveled.

There was someone out there, just through the mist, not very far away. That was why Vivi couldn't speak. Most likely, whoever was grumbling out there had just passed Vivi's hiding spot after traveling up behind her.

Llenn crouched even tighter behind the truck and glanced back the way she came. She spotted a figure coming through the mist.

It was just a bit over twenty yards away. As the man hurried closer, his silhouette gradually took on more detail, until it belonged to an actual person.

That's...one of the T-S armor guys! Llenn thought, startled by the moment of recognition.

Just sixty feet away, a man covered in sci-fi body armor was loudly swearing, "What's the point of these stupid rules?! Screw that author! This is dumb!" For some reason, he didn't have a gun in his hands or anywhere else on his person.

He was on Team T-S, a group with a rather unique personal history.

In their first appearance in SJ2, they took advantage of some long-range shooting to pick off Llenn and Fukaziroh, exhausted after their long battle with the terrible Pitohui, and seize the victory.

In SJ3, all the members aside from Ervin, who was chosen to be on the betrayers' team, got stuck on top of a building as the sea level rose. They thought the cruise ship was coming over to save them, but instead it smashed through the building and drowned them all. That was Pitohui's work.

In SJ4, their defensive power kept them alive for a while, and they even worked together with LPFM for a bit. And in the playtest before that, too.

Because of their helmets, they were largely unreadable people, but from what Llenn remembered, they were veterans of Squad Jam who were pretty decent at fighting.

"Dumbass! Piece of crap! You freakin' loser! Show yourself, sponsor! Do it, coward!" he shouted, announcing his presence to anyone around, without a weapon in his hands. It was as if he'd given up on playing the game at all. Something about it seemed off.

But now that he was unaware of them, and passing by Llenn just thirty feet away, this would be the best chance to get rid of him.

T-S's defense was tremendous, thanks to their body armor, but as Pitohui once said, all armor has softer parts to allow for flexibility.

Those spots were under the arms, the underside of the knees and elbows, and around the neck and throat.

If she stuck her Vorpal Bunnies up against those spots and fired them at the same time, she could deal some serious damage. Just sneak up behind him after he passed, with one shot to the back of each knee. When he fell over, stick the guns against the back of his neck, with another shot each. Or more, if needed.

That would work. She could do it. She could kill him.

Llenn was good at assassination-style PKing. It was all she did when she first started playing *GGO*. Yeah, she was crazy.

If you can kill 'em, kill 'em when the killing's good, and bathe in their blood, she haiku'd violently. There were no seasonal words in that haiku.

"One of the T-S guys is approaching, shouting real loud," Llenn reported to Vivi in her tiniest voice, feeling the bloodlust surge.

"That's a trap," came her response at once.

"Don't make any noise and don't move. Let them all pass," Vivi said.

All? Llenn wondered, picking up on that part. Her confusion lasted only a moment.

She made sure her pink legs were hidden below her poncho behind the truck and wriggled underneath it to hide.

Now she was perfectly hidden, she believed. If they spotted her here, she'd have no choice but to blast them.

She hid her presence by believing she was part of the truck. It was like that thing hunters do, "turning into" trees in order to trick the animals into walking past. Probably.

"Geez, man! Shit! What's with these stupid suburbs? Is every single person who lives out here rich? I'm so jealous!" the T-S man bellowed from the heart, thirty feet away. She held her breath as he passed.

She could see the ID number *06* on his helmet as he stomped up to the T-intersection.

"Dammit! Now the road's out? Which way do I go? Fine... guess I'll go right! Are you happy?! I'm goin' right because I'm right-handed! I love right!" he shouted, and Llenn realized what he was doing.

The T-S member walking at the head of the group had one or more friends he'd met in the mist, and they were following behind him. He was making lots of noise so that he would draw attention and possibly get shot at. If someone attacked him, his friends would jump on them at once.

It was quite a bold strategy, utilizing the full power of T-S's body armor.

The reason he wasn't carrying his gun was probably to play up his frustrated act, to make any attackers think he wouldn't be able to hurt them back, and most importantly of all, so that he didn't have to worry about it being destroyed by a sudden hail of bullets.

Since he'd run out of good reasons for shouting, he had moved on to simply complaining about the rules and whatever else crossed his mind at the moment, including mansions and rich people. These complaints also included information for the companions behind him, who were probably hooked up via comm.

Here they come...

As she stayed perfectly still, just one extra part of the truck, Llenn could see a second player approaching in the narrow crack between the ground and her poncho.

Coming up behind the T-S man was a tall person dressed in brown desert camo and a heavyset man wearing jeans and a leather jacket, like some kind of Western gunslinger.

The two of them were heading down the middle of the wide

road, side by side at a distance of thirty feet from each other. Their movements were careful and quiet, listening for any sign of enemies.

Naturally, they each had their guns at the ready on their right sides, while their eyes swiveled left and right. They had their shooting fingers outstretched, not on the trigger. This was to keep themselves from creating bullet lines—and for general safety—but they would be ready to shoot the moment trouble arose.

On the right side of the road, farther away from Llenn, was the man in desert camo. He was carrying a heavily customized AKM assault rifle. It had a silencer attached, with its original stock and grip switched out, plus added sights and lights and such.

Ultimately, all of those additions and modifications probably increased its size by 50 percent and doubled its weight. It really told you what a total gun freak this guy was.

The Western gunslinger closer to Llenn was holding an angular, futuristic H&K UMP45 submachine gun, which was a total mismatch for his time-specific clothing. This one had a normal setup, but he, too, had attached a bulky silencer to the muzzle.

The silencers were clearly intended to help them eliminate any prey caught by T-S's lure and allow them to continue hunting undetected.

If Llenn got into a firefight with them using nothing but her pistols, she would lose very fast. If she'd attacked the T-S guy without hearing Vivi out, she would have promptly been eliminated.

The danger was perilously deadly, thought Llenn redundantly, part of the truck now. She watched the men go in silence.

They didn't have time to check every detail around them; they were only lurking behind to jump on anyone who fell for the T-S trap. They stayed on the move to ensure they didn't lose sight of the first man.

I am a truck. I am part of the truck. No one will ever confuse me for anything other than the truck. There is no need to waste your bullets shooting at me, she chanted in her head.

"Get out of your mansion, you Richie Riches! I'll destroy your dumb rules! Obey the rules of Squad Jam, sponsor!"

T-S's weird sloganeering chants started to fade as he moved onward, and the pair of menacing men behind him also vanished through the thick mist, silent as ghosts.

"The other two are gone...," Llenn murmured.

"That's good," said Vivi casually, which Llenn heard in person.

"Huh?"

She slowly got up and saw that Vivi was right there, in a half crouch, five yards away. She'd been following behind the two, just far enough that they couldn't see her through the mist, and approached Llenn without drawing her notice, either.

She'd stashed the RPD in her inventory at some point, because it wasn't visible now. Instead, she was holding an M17 pistol. There was a cylindrical silencer on the end of the barrel.

"Were you going to quietly take those two guys out...?" Llenn asked, surprised.

"Only if they realized you were Llenn."

"I see..."

If they'd spotted Llenn, with her massive bounty, the two would have opened fire and never stopped. She would probably—no, certainly—have died. They'd hit her with so many bullets, she would die three times over.

And in that time, Vivi would have snuck up from behind them and quietly taken the two out. She would never have bothered to protect Llenn.

Llenn could feel nothing but amazement at Vivi's ability to quietly yet skillfully prepare for the next step at all times.

Pitohui, too, was a player with excellent foresight, but she was also prone to wild mood swings and destructive impulses. She would sometimes engage in preposterous acts for the fun of it. That was part of her strength as a player.

Vivi, meanwhile, was calm and collected from start to finish, as intelligent and methodical as a chess player. She ensured that no matter what, neither she nor her teammates took any unnecessary damage. Just like during the Five Ordeals.

I see… No wonder Fuka was so impressed.

"I see… No wonder Fuka was so impressed," she said, accidentally speaking her thoughts out loud.

Behind her smartglasses, Vivi blinked with surprise. "She said that? Really? I'm amazed."

"You are?"

"I think Fuka is actually much stronger than me."

"Can I tell her you said that?" Llenn asked. She didn't get to hear the answer.

The sound of gunfire filled the world.

"!"

"Oh!"

Llenn and Vivi promptly did what any *GGO* player who hears gunshots does: They hit the ground.

You could survive most of the gunfights in the world as long as you got down on the ground. That's what Llenn believed, anyway.

An abrupt and quite frenzied gun battle broke out at a fair distance, a mixed performance of different kinds of guns.

There were about five separate types of gunfire, differing in sound, intensity, and rhythm, coming from a distance of between fifty and a hundred yards. M's lessons about telling the distance and direction of gunfire hadn't failed Llenn yet. It was coming from the southeast, where the three men had just gone.

"Someone took the bait," Vivi said happily.

She'd already returned the pistol and its silencer to the holster on her belt and placed the RPD light machine gun on the road. Impressive efficiency. She must have waved her hand to call up the menu while flat on her face and done all the necessary actions while Llenn wasn't watching. Vivi was someone with a great mind for multitasking.

"Let's put some distance between us and them."

"Roger," said Llenn, checking her watch. It was close to 1:27.

In a little over three minutes, the scan would begin, but this fight wasn't going to last that long. At that point, Llenn's location would be revealed to the winner, and they'd realize she was *that close* the whole time. Better to distance themselves now while they had the chance.

Once she was certain there was no one else around, Llenn got to her feet.

A hundred yards was certainly close enough to catch a stray bullet from a nearby firefight. So she made sure no bullet lines were swinging her way, then headed for the left fork of the intersection, to the northwest.

It was taking her away from SHINC's direction, but that would just have to wait. Survival came first.

The raucous sounds of battle were still audible. They never stopped. The rattle of guns was like a drumroll, keeping a ceaseless beat.

Llenn suspected that someone—or some*ones*—noticed T-S but did not realize he was a lure and opened fire. T-S took the shots without flinching, and his two backups retaliated.

But because of the mist, the battle wasn't resolving itself. Perhaps they were all running around and shooting in the direction of the nearest bullet line, unaware of who was friend or foe.

She continued down the road, putting more distance between herself and the fight. No need to get involved, thank you very much. And she made it quick, knowing more enemies could be approaching, drawn by the sound.

"Are you keeping up, Vivi?" she asked her temporary partner, who was presumably following in the mist.

"Yep, no problem."

"That's goo—"

But she couldn't finish that sentence because she was interrupted by something coming through the veil.

It took shape as soon as she saw it and was gone just as quickly, the same way as when she encountered the NSS member while sprinting down the highway.

But this time it went faster. She didn't recognize what she had just seen until half a second after it was gone.

"Ah."

Just after Llenn recognized it, it must have passed Vivi behind her.

"Ah."

She made the exact same sound just a moment later.

"Aaah! Run as fast as you can! Follow my light!" Llenn cried, sticking the Vorpal Bunnies into their holsters and breaking into a run. Her pace was just slow enough that she thought Vivi would be able to keep up.

"Got it," said Vivi's voice in her ear.

She didn't know if the other girl was actually keeping up, but they were running on a paved surface. The IR strobe light and smartglasses would surely be enough for her to see Llenn.

Crap, crap, crap, crap, crap, CRAP, CRAP, CRAP!

Her pulse was racing like a jackrabbit, or like the automatic gunfire she could still hear in the distance.

The *thing* she saw for just a moment…

For just a split second, but quite clearly enough to make out. There was no doubt…

It was…

A player on a bicycle.

There had been a mountain bike somewhere on the map, which a player found and was now riding at breakneck speed. It was basically as fast as Llenn at her absolute limit.

And Llenn recognized the general look of the player. It was someone she had seen before in person, not on a recording. Someone she had seen in the last Squad Jam.

Their team wore all kinds of bulky armor, but on the front only, plus a helmet, so they looked like giant tin robot toys. On the other side, they carried huge backpacks.

He was with them! DOOM, the suicide bomb squad!

She couldn't help but feel her hair stand on end.

They had nearly wiped out Llenn's team right at the start of SJ4, in their very first appearance in the event. DOOM wore armor only on their front side and would approach any enemy, even through gunfire if necessary. Once in range, they blew themselves up with the high-grade explosives in their backpacks. It was the ultimate offensive team.

They would never win on their own, but in terms of their ability to cause havoc, none were more dangerous. They were basically terrorists capable of completely destroying even a heavy favorite.

And from personal experience in SJ4, Llenn knew their explosive power was nothing to scoff at. From watching the video after the event, M surmised that anyone caught within a radius of fifty yards would be annihilated, even if you were behind cover. The ripples from the shockwave alone would turn your internal organs to mush.

And if you needed more than that, without seriously heavy protection like concrete walls, the force would send you flying far enough to potentially cause fatal damage all on its own.

On top of that, the blast winds carried even farther, so if anything was blown up between you and the blast, it would be turned into lethal shrapnel, just like in a hurricane or tornado.

If M hadn't overturned the trailer in SJ4 and the sturdy vehicle (plus iron beams) hadn't shielded them, LPFM would have been blown to kingdom come. Or at least, all the way off the bridge.

What Llenn was thinking about—was terrified of—was *where* the man on the bicycle was going to explode.

If he rode right into the middle of the firefight and detonated, that would be nice. But it might be too optimistic.

If he blew up by the closest enemy to Llenn and Vivi, it was a sure thing that they would be significantly hurt by it, too.

And while it might have been a figment of her imagination, the backpack he was carrying sure seemed larger than the last time.

But maybe it's just a figment of my imagination. I sure hope it is. It sure better be!

As she ran, Llenn said, "That guy was on the self-destructing team last time! We gotta put some distance between us, or we'll get yeeted right off the map!"

"Spoken like a true zoomer."

"That's not important right now!"

"Then let me say what *is* important. Slow down a little bit. I can't catch up to you. I'll lose sight of you."

"Ugh..."

Llenn had shifted into a full sprint without realizing it. Chagrined, she slowed back down.

She couldn't see anyone in the mist, but if she did run across them, she'd immediately shout, "Hey, you! It's dangerous this way. Turn around!"

The sound of the firefight was getting quieter. No explosions yet.

There you go. Don't explode. Don't explode, don't explode, don't you dare explode.

He exploded.

CHAPTER 5
Converging

CHAPTER 5
Converging

The attack came from behind.

The world beyond her back turned orange, and the ground beneath Llenn's feet rumbled before she heard the sound. Then the shock wave lifted her tiny body into the air.

"Fwee?"

She flew.

It was as though she'd been launched by a catapult. Her brain experienced a virtual sensation of acceleration g's like nothing she had ever felt before.

There had been a sound apparently, but it was so huge, and she was so preoccupied being tumbled like a piece of laundry in a washing machine, that Llenn couldn't have said if she actually heard it or not.

As she spun and her mind focused, stretching the moment into slow motion, she could see a single mansion.

It was an impressive structure, built of red brick and sturdier than the others around it.

Unlike the others in the neighborhood, this one was two stories. The sloped wooden roof contained a truly majestic chimney that could have fit three Santas at once.

As it came back around into view with each rotation of her

body, the building grew larger, like she was seeing it through stop-motion animation, and she could tell she was shooting toward it like a bullet.

She was going to hit it in a moment. It was like she was "falling" toward it, just at a ninety-degree angle.

Oh, I'm dead. Deader than dead, Llenn thought but did not say aloud. She couldn't have, even if she wanted to. She couldn't even tell if she was breathing, virtual world or not.

But even if I die, there's something I can do while I have time left! Llenn thought, determined to make one final act of resistance.

She twisted her body in midair, flailing her arms and bending her knees, doing whatever she could to alter her balance and change her rotation so that her back was facing the house. She was like a satellite, using her arms to control her balance.

And if possible, she was trying to go through a big window, rather than hitting a brick wall.

Llenn's desperate resistance, thanks to her incredible agility stat, or perhaps thanks to her natural reflexes—or both—paid off in the end.

Her tiny body managed to change its angle and posture just slightly. But even a small change could lead to big differences when you were speeding at an incredible rate. She changed course like a breaking ball thrown by a fireballing pitcher.

Just after her final rotation came to a gentle halt, Llenn slammed through the middle of a large window back-first.

The living room window shattered into pieces, allowing the small white-camo-poncho-covered form a most dynamic entrance to the room.

"Hyaaa!"

Llenn flew through the middle of the room until she hit the tattered, fancy couch there, butt-first, and bounced off.

"Whoa!"

The blast followed her inside the house, jarring everything loose and sending her into one last backflip, so she hit her back against the wall above the fireplace, then fell downward into a sitting position on the mantel.

"Whoa..."

Her vision was woozy as a result of the experience, but at least she had stopped moving.

Dreading what she would see, she checked her hit point bar. Sure enough, she had taken damage: about 30 percent.

But after being blasted dozens of yards away, she had to consider it a major victory that she hadn't taken any more than that. She was still the lucky girl, it turned out.

And then she could see.

"Whoa..."

It was bright.

Beyond the room—which was dancing with dust, scraps of paper, and any other light thing that could float—outside the broken window, the sky was clear.

Like the usual *GGO*, it was a reddish-blue sky. Ahhh, what a clear day. It felt quite refreshing to see.

She could also see very far—three hundred yards, in fact—and very clearly through the neighborhood, which was now full of half-destroyed houses.

The world that had been totally shrouded in mist was instantly cleared up.

It's sunny? Why? Llenn wondered, but the answer came to her almost immediately.

It was because there was a massive gray mushroom cloud rising toward the blue sky above the ruined residential block.

Oh, it blew away the mist...

The incredible pressure of the explosion, which was indeed

significantly increased in size since SJ4, had temporarily cleared away the mist for several hundred yards around, making the world instantly more visible.

Awww...it's so beautiful, Llenn thought before recalling that there was something else to check on first.

"Vivi? Are you all right?"

She had been far behind Llenn and must have taken much more of the violent blast. Although, with as big as it was, maybe the difference between their positions was minimal.

"I am...alive," said her voice. She had not been knocked out of Squad Jam.

But she sounded fatigued. She was normally so reserved and graceful, but her voice sounded practically gloomy now.

Llenn hopped down from the mantel and said, "Where are you? I'm in a big redbrick house."

"I can see it. The visibility is very clear now."

"Can you make it over?"

"I can't."

Llenn figured it out. Vivi was in very bad condition at the moment.

Trapped under rubble? Stuck between things? Sprained ankle? Or even worse, missing a few limbs?

She didn't know why Vivi couldn't move, but she knew there was one thing she could do.

"I'll go help you! Where are you?" Llenn said, jumping out the same window she flew through, right as a gust of wind and rumbling noise blew past.

"Pwah!"

Her poncho whipped and struggled wildly around her.

The stormy gust was dragging her forward from behind. Thanks to the massive building behind her, she was surely being spared from the worst of it.

It was the blast wind, sucking the air back into the low-pressure center.

White misty air surrounded Llenn, stealing her visibility again.

All of the charred buildings around the blast center, the empty foundations of structures totally demolished, and the blackened road were totally blocked by the fogginess once again.

Everyone who had been in there was certainly dead. It was just too far for her to see any of the DEAD tags in the air.

"Can you come right to me?"

"Okay!"

Llenn started running into the wind. The return of the mist was a good thing for them. It would hide Llenn in her white camo poncho and also hide Vivi, where she was currently immobile.

"You'll have to give me directions, since I can't see you. Am I getting closer?" she asked.

Vivi watched her infrared strobe light and said, "You're fine. A bit farther to the left. Yes, now you're in front of me."

"Got it."

Llenn proceeded over dirt littered with small pieces of wood. This was the yard of the huge mansion. It took her about fifteen seconds to cross the distance that she'd flown in just two or three.

During that time, the mist flowed back into the world, and the wind quickly died down.

She hurried along, avoiding or kicking the pieces of wood in her way, and eventually came to a fence.

It was a sturdy metal fence painted black, marking the property line between mansions. The bars on the fence were not rounded, but square, a bit more than an inch wide on each side. They were spaced about a foot apart, and each one was topped with a decorative point like the spade symbol from a deck of cards. The fence was easily over ten feet tall. It was like the fence around a prison.

Llenn was used to seeing fences like this in *GGO*. It was a commonly used bit of set design in the residential areas of the game.

They offered a clear view through and wouldn't stop a bullet, and yet they were very hard to get past. On top of that, they often continued on and on, so players hated them, by and large.

If you had a plasma grenade, however, the spherical explosion would eat right through the bars, allowing you passage. It came in handy when there weren't any enemies around.

Item damage was handled very carefully and specifically in *GGO*. In most cases, when something was broken, *only* the broken part would be affected.

In other games, when an item's durability reached zero, the item would simply vanish in its entirety. In *GGO*, an item above a certain size would generally only break *where it broke*, and everything else would retain its proper shape.

This was why you could put a hole in a wall, and the wall itself wouldn't simply vanish. Same thing for fences. It was said that this happened because *GGO* was fixated on re-creating the realistic sensations of doing battle in post-apocalyptic ruins—that it was a result of pursuing the beauty of destruction—but it wasn't clear if this was true or not.

Llenn reached the fence and was just wondering where Vivi was, when she heard her voice say, "Oh dear."

"Huh?" Llenn looked in the direction she heard the voice come from: upward.

And she was shocked into silence.

"…!"

She'd been so focused on the ground beneath her feet to keep from falling that she'd never noticed on her approach.

Vivi was on top of the fence…

…with the sharpened points digging into her stomach.

* * *

"Wha—?! Huh?! Are you...?"

Are you all right? she wanted to ask but realized that it was pointless. Instead, she tried to grasp the situation.

Three of the pointed spades at the top of the fence's bars were stuck in Vivi's body.

One was deep enough through her lower left flank that it burst out the back side. She was totally skewered.

One was high on the right side of her stomach, vanishing into her body just below the lung. It went through the thick fabric of her chest rig, too.

One was jabbed into her left thigh. This one was only the tip, but even still, it was an inch or two in there.

Spades were meant to symbolize the pike, and they were certainly displaying that quality here. Vivi was facedown and slightly bent, suspended ten feet off the ground, completely immobilized.

Even if she wanted to pry herself off the points with her limbs, the crossbar was too close to her body; she couldn't apply enough force to leverage herself up. And below that, it was nothing but vertical bars, with nothing to push against.

But even beyond that, if she tried to move herself, it was likely to just shift her weight farther downward.

It was like the sort of thing that shrikes did to their smaller prey, impaling them on sharp branch points. All Llenn could think when she looked at Vivi was, *The poor thing...*

Just to be clear, *GGO* is a game about having fun killing other people with guns, as well as other means. Like many other players, Llenn had pressed her gun to people's heads and blasted them through, had blown them to pieces with a well-aimed grenade, and had torn vertically through a man's groin with a knife.

Okay, maybe *only* Llenn had done that last one.

But these were all things that you would never expect to see happen when you lived in peaceful Japan. They were so unreal, so beyond the scope of reality, that the shock of them didn't really register.

So in comparison, seeing Vivi's current state, something tragically horrific that *could* possibly happen, was much worse.

How did this happen?

Until the blast had hit them, she'd been with Llenn.

But Vivi had been knocked high into the air and, through some twist of fate, had landed right here on top of the fence stomach-first.

Her RPD fell over ten yards away on the other side of the fence. It looked lonely and forlorn in the misty distance. Hopefully it wasn't broken.

"Of all the terrible luck… Ouch," Vivi hissed weakly.

Of course, pain in *GGO* was nothing like pain in the real world, but there was no way that the sensation of having something virtually jammed through your torso was pleasant.

Llenn asked the most important question: "How are your hit points?"

She couldn't be fine. Was it 20 percent down or 30? And if she was impaled, that meant she had to be continually losing more with every second.

"The moment I landed, I was down to half. Now I'm at twenty percent left."

"Yikes!" Llenn blanched. Her guess had turned out to be extremely optimistic.

If left on her own, Vivi would run out of health in less than a minute. She was going to die, and her SJ5 would be over.

At that moment, Llenn's wristwatch vibrated, and she glanced at the time. It was 1:29:30. Thirty-one. Thirty-two.

In just twenty seconds, the third Satellite Scan would start, and all ammo would be replenished, but there was no time to check the map now.

There was a more important task at hand. She had to save her suffering comrade.

"Emergency med kit!"

"I can't reach it."

"I'll do it! Where?"

"Left thigh pocket."

"Got it!"

Llenn quickly jumped onto the bars. Holding one bar in each hand and using the soles of her boots to launch herself upward, she quickly shimmied up. She was climbing as fast as a monkey. Even faster, in fact.

When she was little, in terms of age and size, Llenn had climbed lots of trees with her siblings. Who would have guessed that it would come in handy here? The skill came right back to her, like riding a bicycle.

"Oh my goodness," remarked Vivi at the sight of Llenn zipping up the bars.

She reached for Vivi's left pocket. The spade stabbing her thigh right in front of that spot was horrendous to look at. The red of the bullet hole—er, fence hole?—glowed intensely.

Llenn carefully pulled out the med kit, which looked like a fat pen, and stuck it into Vivi's leg.

"Thank you."

Vivi's body glowed, and her hit points began to recover. The problem was that it would heal only 30 percent of her maximum health. And it would take three minutes to finish.

At this stage, it was doing nothing more than prolonging her death for a few moments.

"Well, I'd really like to pull you off of there..."

But Llenn knew it would be impossible with her strength. She simply couldn't imagine using one hand to lift the skewered Vivi up off the spikes. She probably wouldn't be strong enough even with both hands.

"Do you have a plasma grenade?"

That blue spherical surge would do the trick. But she had a feeling Vivi didn't have one. If she did, she would have dropped it already.

"Unfortunately, no," came the answer Llenn expected.

Arrrgh! If only Pito or Fuka were here! she thought.

"Arrrgh! If only Pito or Fuka were here!" she shouted out loud.

"Well...it's not going to work. I suppose this is it for me. You go on ahead."

"......"

That might be the logical conclusion.

The massive explosion probably scared everyone off, but there was no guarantee other enemies wouldn't converge on this spot, and if that happened, the two were sitting ducks.

Perhaps Llenn should just go on and survive on her own. That's what kind of game Squad Jam was anyway.

"In that case," Llenn said, making up her mind with a smirk, "I'll keep trying until it's over."

She let go of the bars and kicked off the fence. As she floated through the air, she waved her hand to bring up the menu, then hit the equipment switch button.

The backpack that had been protecting her vanished, as did the Vorpal Bunnies and their holsters. When she landed, the P90 was forming right before her eyes.

The familiar shape was a mixture of straight lines, curved lines, and some other kinds of lines she couldn't describe. You might say it had functional beauty, or you might not, but in any case, it was a shape Llenn was very fond of. It was also pink, the color she chose to paint it.

Don't even have twenty seconds left!

Llenn grabbed the P90 and sent the first bullet into the firing chamber by pulling and releasing the loading lever.

Vivi replied by asking weakly, "Trying what?"

The vertical bars were about a foot apart. There were three consecutive bars skewering Vivi.

Here goes, P-chan! Show off your blade! Or your fangs! Or whatever!

"*You got it! Let me handle this!*" said the P90 in its energetic, boyish voice.

Llenn pointed the gun at one of the bars. If she stuck it right against the metal, it might deflect the bullet back, so she gave it a few inches of space.

Bratta-ratta-ratta-ratta-ratta-ratta!

The P90 spat fire for the first time this game, and the collision of bullets and metal bars sent up sparks.

The bullets were very small and light, less than a tenth of an ounce, but when delivered at supersonic speed, even a metal bar would suffer. And this was fifteen bullets a second.

The gun fired so fast that the shots sounded like one continuous sound. Empty cartridges glittered as they flew out of the bottom of the gun, then glittered again when they vanished from the game.

With each hit, the bar bent and warped, until at last it snapped in two.

"That's one!"

Llenn checked the ammo counter in the bottom right of her vision. The P90 had a magazine capacity of fifty, and there were still over thirty shots remaining. She set about to sever the next bar.

Another round of automatic fire.

P-chan growled. Sparks and empties flew.

She was getting the hang of it. The second one snapped quite easily.

"That's two!"

Watching from ten feet off the ground, Vivi asked her, "Did they teach you how to do that in the manual?"

"Nope!"

Llenn continued, determined to use all the bullets in her magazine.

There was a third series of sparks and gunshots. *Sorry for the distraction, everyone trying to work nearby. Almost done.*

"Got it!"

The third bar snapped. Only the horizontal bar was left.

There was no time to pay any attention to the surroundings. Llenn performed a blindingly fast magazine change, bumping the P90's ammo counter up to fifty-one. Fifty in the magazine—one in the chamber.

She propped the P90 against her shoulder and then monkey-climbed back up to Vivi. It was frustrating that even having snapped off the roots of the columns, the horizontal bar was still holding them firmly in place.

"How much left?"

"Ten percent, maybe?"

With that cleared up, Llenn used her empty left hand and her feet to hold herself steady, then used the P90 with her right hand to shoot.

She started with the right side of the bar. The gunshots and sparks sprayed, gouging away at the two-inch-thick bar, which eventually snapped.

"Whoa!"

"Urgh!"

The next moment, the top of the fence bent downward, along with Vivi.

Llenn was left hanging from nothing but her left hand, while Vivi and the piece of fencing hung at an angle, though not far enough to snap off the other end.

"Why, you..."

The fence was Llenn's archenemy, her biggest foe in Squad Jam to date. She stretched with her right arm and managed to point the muzzle of the gun at the spot where the horizontal bar was bent.

"Take thiiiiis!"

She fired and fired and fired.

It took all her focus to keep the recoil under control so that the gun still pointed at the target. It was a very unbalanced posture, so several of the bullets simply vanished into the mist and beyond.

The world was full of sparks and gunshots and cartridges, until the horizontal bar suddenly and mercifully lost its purpose.

"Hya!"

Vivi was free from the bar—and trapped in gravity's clutches.

She entered free fall from ten feet up, along with the fence stuck in her.

Oh no, she might die from the fall! Llenn thought, terrified, as she hung from the fence with one hand. But it was too late for that. There was no other way to do it anyway.

Don't die, at least!

Vivi plunged toward the ground, turning horizontal, with the metal bars stuck in her abdomen and leg.

"Whoa, there!"

She landed in a pair of burly arms, which belonged to a burly voice.

Since she hadn't been looking down or around, Llenn had never seen the player running toward them. She had no idea.

Then she saw who it was: someone she'd been hoping to see.

"Boss!"

"Yo! You've been through quite an ordeal!"

There was a pigtailed gorilla dressed in speckled green camo below, looking up at Llenn with a smile that would cause little children to burst into tears.

Her signature gun, the VSS Vintorez silenced sniper rifle, was slung over her back.

"There we go," she said, and with a motion like lifting a baby, she held Vivi up with one hand and pulled out the spears impaling her with the other. It was like pulling the skewers out of a piece of grilled chicken.

Within moments, all three were out, and she set Vivi gently on the dirt.

Vivi looked up at the massive gorilla from the ground and said, "Oh, thank you. I've never seen my hit point bar so close to empty. Thank you both."

The fact that she wasn't dead meant her hit points had stopped decreasing. Thanks to the med kit, in fact, they were recovering. Unless she took on fresh damage—like, say, if Boss rolled over on top of her and crushed her, in which case she might die—Vivi would be fine.

"I'm so glaaaad!" Llenn wailed, hopping off the top of the fence and paying close attention to ensure she wouldn't accidentally land on Vivi.

But before she landed, she spotted a man in the distance holding a Swiss SIG SG 550 assault rifle and screeching, "Lucky meeee!"

The man, whose clothes and face were familiar, stood out against the thick fog about twenty yards away, pointing his gun at them. He must have heard Llenn shooting, thought it was a battle, and crawled up to get a closer look.

Since the three of them were preoccupied and weren't in any position to counterattack, he must have stood up for a more comfortable aim.

Knowing that one of his three targets was worth an incredible amount of money, it was no wonder he was feeling lucky.

I get it. I really, really get it.

But despite the pinpoint accuracy of her instantaneous guess, Llenn was unable to counterattack. He started firing before she could aim and fire the P90. He was going to riddle her and Boss and Vivi with bullets and knock all three of them out of SJ5.

Would you at least shoot me first? Llenn prayed.

Since she was the smallest target, maybe he would miss a few shots, so Boss would actually have enough time to do something—if not while Llenn was alive, then while she was dead.

She hit the ground, staring down the barrel of the gun the man was about to fire at her.

"Hagk!"

He suddenly lurched backward and toppled to the ground.

She could see the glowing red dot on his face, which made it obvious he'd been shot.

Bing.

The DEAD tag appeared instantly over the spot where he fell. It had been a fatal headshot.

Very well done.

It wasn't much fun as a game if people just died immediately, so the range of insta-kill points was actually quite narrow in *GGO*.

It depended on the power of the bullet you used, of course—but for a normal assault rifle, you couldn't deliver that kind of instantaneous death, not even allowing a pull of the trigger in response, unless your shot went right through the brain stem.

But where did it come from? Who did it? I didn't hear any shots, Llenn thought as she lowered her P90.

"Oh. So it was you guys," said a man's familiar voice behind her.

Llenn spun around and matched the sound to the face she saw.

"Ohhh!"

Standing about twenty yards away, covered by a light layer of mist, was a man holding a Steyr STM-556 assault rifle, with a silencer attached, plus a grenade launcher.

He wore green camo in a blocky geometric pattern, featuring a shoulder patch of a skull holding a knife in its mouth: the leader of his team, David.

It was 1:32.

The four of them—Llenn, Vivi, Boss, and David—were on the second floor of the huge brick mansion Llenn had been blasted into earlier.

For their present needs, it was actually quite a lovely location to occupy.

The walls were all sturdy brick, which would make it difficult for any bullets to get through. Even bricks would chip away if shot consecutively, so it wasn't perfectly safe. But a wall of multiple layers of brick wouldn't let any initial shot through, or a second, or a third. Although an ultrapowerful antitank rifle or antimateriel rifle would probably do the trick.

If this were your typical two-by-four wood construction seen in America, the walls would be very thin. Rifle rounds would cut right through the structure on the first shot.

Thanks to *GGO*, Llenn had learned that being inside a house or vehicle did not make you safe from military rifles. It was the kind of knowledge she didn't know how to make use of in the real world.

On top of that, it was a two-story structure, so they had a vantage point of several yards higher than anyone else.

The mist was still thick, and it was hard to tell what was more than thirty yards away. Still, having better visibility and verticality than being on the ground was an unquestionable advantage.

In combat, whoever had the high ground had an overwhelming edge. This was something Llenn had learned in *GGO.* Again, not something she knew how to make use of in real life.

The four of them were in different rooms.

There were rooms that faced north, south, east, and west on the second floor, so they each took one. Boss was in the east room, Vivi was in the west, Llenn was in the south, and David was in the north.

They peered out the windows there, covering each cardinal direction. The interior of the house was a wreck, to the point that it was hard to imagine anyone had ever lived there, but at least the floor was sturdy.

Once they were all in place and could confirm that nothing was out of the ordinary outside, Vivi said, "Let me thank the three of you again. Llenn for the great idea, Eva for the nice catch, and David for the superb headshot."

Her voice was gentle and genuine. Of course, they were all using the comm, which they'd connected to one another.

"You're welcome," said Llenn sprightly.

"Believe it or not, I'm good at catching people. I'm glad it came in handy," said Boss happily; she was a gymnast in real life.

"Look…it just worked out that way. You don't need to thank me," said David, refusing her sentiment. But he certainly sounded pleased. He just couldn't hide his true feelings.

"Now, as for the scan," he continued.

Two minutes ago, the third Satellite Scan passed, and he was the only one who got to see it. Llenn and Boss were too busy guarding Vivi with their bodies and focusing on the surroundings, since a single bullet, or even a good graze, would have killed her.

"There were no leader dots within two-thirds of a mile of us. Of course, that doesn't mean there are no *enemies* that close. There were still thirty dots, meaning no teams have been collectively wiped out yet. In fact, none of the leader dots moved much at all."

Interesting, interesting.

That told Llenn that Boss wasn't the leader of SHINC. It was probably Tanya, the speediest.

David, too, had given the leadership role to someone else. He probably decided he wanted to be a free-roaming soldier so that he could help trick opponents and ambush them.

Llenn had her P90—with all ammo refilled—propped against the side of the window, with her eye keenly watching the ground outside. Her hit points were recovering, thanks to the med kit she'd used. It should bring her back up to 100 percent. And none of her teammates were dead.

"You're the leader of LPFM, right? So they know you're here. But it's not a bad spot," David had said. And he was right.

If you were going to stay put and defend a position, this was a great one to choose. With a few exceptions in terms of enemies.

"If another one of those explosive freaks from before shows up, we'll be screwed."

Yes, *those* guys. Because of the thick mist, it was impossible to keep them a long distance away from you. And once they were close, they were invincible. DOOM still had up to five members remaining.

Boss said, "Even still, let's wait here until Vivi's back to normal."

While she was recovering, Vivi's remaining hit points were still low, and it would be dangerous to let her go out into the open.

"Agreed!" said Llenn.

"Got it," said David.

"Thank you all again," said Vivi.

And that was how the four of them agreed to put down roots and watch their perimeter. They were going to hold down the fort.

With their strategy decided and her position secured, Llenn went ahead and asked what she wanted to know. "Boss, what have you guys been doing?"

"Well, once these shitty rules were revealed, we planned on survival, nothing more. We said, 'Let's stay in place and hide until two o'clock, no matter what.' In fact, I ordered the team to do that. I started from this residential block."

"Oh, I see."

So by coincidence, Boss's starting point hadn't been that far away from Llenn's. Their unified map data, which popped up once they were standing next to each other, proved as much. The only thing it added to Llenn's map was a bit more of the neighborhood.

She'd also gotten map data from the three players who tried to run her over, but she still had less than 10 percent of the map overall.

Despite knowing she was fairly close to Llenn, Boss had been disciplined enough to stick to her words and stay put. After all, if she'd gone chasing after Llenn and died, it would have been for nothing. And given how fast Llenn was, they could have simply passed each other in the mist without realizing.

"Right at the start, I put down some chairs in the back of one of these houses and hid. And around twenty minutes in, someone actually snuck inside."

"And that was David?"

"No. It was one of the all-optical team guys that keeps entering Squad Jams. I was thinking I'd take him out, but he wouldn't come into a position where I could get out my gun and aim. I could have used a pistol, but I didn't want to make noise. Eventually, he just started hanging out at the window and made himself at home. It was a real pain."

She could have taken him out with a single shot from the Vintorez, a silenced sniper rifle, without drawing any attention, but only if she could manage to aim it at him.

David explained, "Through some odd twist of fate, I happened to start very close by. And by coincidence, I happened to see him hiding in there. I got in and quietly eliminated him—and the next thing I knew, Eva and I were glaring at each other in the same room."

"I see."

So it was similar to what happened with Llenn and Vivi.

At that close range, it would be a mutual kill at best. So in that situation, better to team up with someone you already knew was talented.

"I wasn't planning to team up with anyone, and I told my teammates the same thing—but I didn't want to die before I could meet up with them… And when I saw Eva leering at me with a grand grenade strapped to her forehead, all I could do was click my tongue with disgust."

"It didn't seem like a proper attitude to exhibit toward a lady," Boss said gleefully.

If David had shot her, the extra-large plasma grenade would have gone off and exploded the entire house.

Boss continued, "We were just going to wait until two o'clock from there, but that mammoth explosion busted up most of the house. We should have taken that bombing team into account from the start. If only I'd picked out a brick house to hide in. Can't believe I forgot the age-old lesson from 'The Three Little Pigs.'"

"Bwa-ha-ha-ha!" Llenn roared.

"So once I managed to dig myself out of the rubble, I heard a P90 going off like crazy. I knew there was a good chance it was you, so I carefully made my approach until I saw you."

"Interesting!"

It was a good thing the house they'd been hiding in was only half-destroyed. If they'd been any closer to the center of the blast, they could have been obliterated along with the house or crushed under the rubble, and that would have been it for the both of them.

Plus, Llenn and Vivi would have gotten shot by that man, and it would be curtains for them, too.

David said, "I know it's a little late for this, but...these are the only two real options for the first hour of this Squad Jam: Either you do nothing and hide on your own, or you find someone else at random and temporarily team up."

"That's right. And three is better than two, so four should be better than three, right?" said Vivi. Llenn and Boss could tell what they were saying.

"Very well," said Boss with a grin, her voice deep and menacing. "The four of us can't possibly find fault in one another's skill."

"No, no, no! Of course not!" insisted Llenn quite sincerely.

The other three were right there among the toughest players in Squad Jam. If anything, she was easily the weakest of the four.

Her wristwatch said it was 1:35.

For the next twenty-five minutes, the four of them could take whatever that nasty sponsor threw at them and survive, easy.

And after all...our real battle starts at the hour! SJ5 begins at two o'clock. We just showed up a little early, that's all.

"Very well. Then with that decided—with that decided... let's...stay here and do what we're doing," said David, who realized belatedly that he had run out of ways to end that sentence.

Llenn had no objections. Camping out in the upstairs of a sturdy building with eyes in all four directions was a huge advantage. Except against antimateriel rifles. And suicide bombers.

However, there was one cause for concern: herself.

"But my location will be known at forty and fifty minutes. I know I pretended to not be participating. But maybe some people weren't aware of our trick."

"Well, we can't do anything about that," said Boss at once. "If it happens, we'll just use you as a marker to lure suckers closer."

What a pal.

"There you have it. I'll heal myself up to sixty percent. But until then, let me take the back-seat role," said Vivi.

She had used her second med kit, then. Even that would only put her a bit short of 60 percent, three minutes from now. She had only one more after this. That was a big blow to suffer right at the start.

David said, "You have a silencer, right, Llenn? Put it on your P90."

"Oh! Roger!"

It was the first time he'd ever given her tactical instructions, but she wasn't going to complain.

Llenn removed the cylinder from her inventory and stuck it onto the muzzle of her P90 to prevent its sounds of battle from spreading far and wide. Like the gun, it was painted pink, of course.

In addition to dampening the sound, the silencer also hid the blazing muzzle flash of the gun, too. That would make it harder for enemies to notice her, even when shooting in the mist. There was no hiding the bullet lines, though.

Of course, such a convenient item did not come without its downsides.

First, it was simply an expensive item to acquire. And having it attached lowered the gun's accuracy.

Most of all, though, it increased the length of the barrel, making the gun less mobile. This was Llenn's least-favorite part of the silencer, since part of the reason she chose the P90 was because of how short it was.

It was best to put it on while they were holed up in here, though. She decided to be good and equip the item.

She felt much more reassured with plenty of companions around.

Llenn thought, *At this point, with this group, I feel like I can easily survive until two o'clock. First, I teamed up with Vivi, and despite some spills, we survived, and then we teamed up with David and Boss, two more powerful players...*

I really am a lucky girl.

That was at the same moment that Boss hissed, "Enemy attack!"

Boss was at the eastern-facing window. Llenn was facing south, so she moved along the windowsill and angled herself so she could look in that direction. Unfortunately, because of the house's construction and the angle, she couldn't see the enemy.

"There are two players running from the east. Neither appears to be a teammate. I don't see anyone else. They're aiming to get inside this house. I'll shoot," Boss reported, firing precise information to the others in a prompt fashion.

If they're not from any of our four teams, then waste 'em, Llenn thought.

"Firing. Two down," Boss reported.

Thanks to the silenced Vintorez, Llenn didn't hear a single sound.

Surely that would mean no one else had realized they were hiding in the building. Yeah, it was still a secret.

The Vintorez had a firing-mode switch that allowed you to use automatic fire, too. Though the range was lower, you could use it as a silenced assault rifle, if you wanted.

Boss must have turned it on full auto and showered the two oncomers with bullets. Llenn had a terrifying run-in with that gun in SJ1, but it was great to have on your own side.

Relieved, Llenn checked her watch again: 1:38.

It's a little early, but I guess I'll prepare to check the next scan, she thought comfortably, just before the building shook.

"Hyeep!"

Some kind of explosion had rocked the brick building. The sound of the blast filled the room.

"Grenade launcher!" said Boss. "It landed below my room. I don't see who—"

Gunfire drowned out her voice. It was a furious machine-gun racket that filled the entire world. Sounds that heavy and that close together could only come from a 7.62 mm machine gun.

"Gah! Pulling back!" Boss exclaimed. Her tone of voice was what caused Llenn to finally realize how serious the situation was.

The machine gun was hitting the east side of the building, it seemed. Llenn could actually feel the vibrations slightly from her room.

"Need backup?"

"No!" said Boss. "Don't lean out toward the east!"

"Wait a moment!" said Vivi in what was a positively panicked voice by her standards. "That's our Shinohara! It's an M60E3!"

Ugh! Llenn thought.

"Ugh!" David yelled out loud.

"Either way, there's no way to get back at him. Do something!" pleaded Boss.

If it was someone from ZEMAL, then his machine gun would be hooked up to the backpack-loading system. That would give him about a thousand bullets he could fire consecutively.

He couldn't actually shoot that long due to barrel overheating, but ZEMAL had more practice switching out barrels than washing their own faces. He could do it in a blink.

Although Llenn couldn't see it, she could envision the situation in her mind's eye.

Boss was hiding in her room, which was under a hail of bullets at the moment. Shinohara must have seen her bullet lines when she shot the other two players. He must have come running right after them.

Thanks to the brick construction, the bullets wouldn't immediately hit every corner of the room, but with that rate of fire, there was no way to peer out the window or stick your gun out to shoot back.

That's not good!

And even if she *could* shoot back, she shouldn't. Shinohara was Vivi's teammate, after all.

If only she were on the east side, she could use the infrared strobe light on the top of her poncho to show Shinohara that she wasn't an enemy, and he wouldn't open fire. What bad luck.

If only she had a time machine, she could have protected the eastern side instead, just a few minutes ago.

"I'll go!" said Vivi's voice.

Llenn couldn't see her, but she must have been crossing the house from the west side. Llenn was on the south side, which was closer to Boss. She wondered if she should go, since she was faster. If she could somehow show off the strobe light, Shinohara should stop shooting.

But since Vivi was already on the way over, she decided not to butt in.

The gunshots continued.

She needed to keep an eye out for new enemies on the south side *and* the west side, now that Vivi wasn't covering it anymore.

No worries, Vivi will solve this one, Llenn thought, but then a different idea occurred to her. *Wait, grenade launcher? That's what Boss said first, right? That first vibration was from a grenade?*

"Vivi! Does Shinohara have a grenade launcher?"

"No. I think he must have teamed up with someone," said Vivi. Of course, she was smart enough to have guessed that.

Shinohara was probably forming a tag team, or perhaps a trio, with someone who had a grenade launcher. But if they showed Shinohara the strobe light, the attack would most likely stop.

He would tell his companion not to attack his own teammate, and if they were a decent player, they would heed his request and stop, too.

"Made it!" said Vivi. She had entered Boss's room. That horrible machine-gun clatter would stop very soon. Please, please let it stop.

Please don't let Shinohara shoot Vivi! Llenn prayed fervently. It would be too tragic to believe.

And just like that—the M60E3 stopped shooting. The world was silent.

In that new, sudden silence, Vivi shouted, "Shinohara! Come and meet up here!"

Llenn heard her through the comm in her left ear and through the air in her right. Apparently, she had an impressive set of lungs on her.

And then, at least as loud: "Ohhhhhhh! Leader! You're in there?! I'm so sorry for shooting at youuuu!"

Shinohara's voice sounded even louder than Vivi's.

Llenn was totally relieved. At the very least, there would be no tragedies of friendly fire.

"I'll go over there now!" Shinohara continued, getting closer. Llenn snuck a look out the window and saw a figure emerge from the mist to the southeast of the building.

Just in case, she pointed her P90 toward him, but made sure not to let her finger touch the trigger.

Sure enough, the man coming through the mist was Shinohara, the member of ZEMAL who had black hair and a headband, just like the hero of a certain action movie. He rushed over, making his way around the rubble from other exploded houses.

"I'm so sorry, Leader! I was following two other players, and I believed they had fled into this house!"

"No, we beat them."

"Understood! You may scold me as much as you want later!"

Uh-huh.

So Shinohara had teamed up with whoever had the grenade launcher and was tracking the two whom Boss had just taken out. He never noticed that the two had died, so he simply assumed that whoever was inside the house was his enemy and started shooting.

Apparently, those two players were running to get away from Shinohara and his friend, then. That was understandable.

Shinohara rushed up to the building, where Llenn could see him.

He was wearing a green fleece jacket with black combat pants, the uniform of his team. His M60E3 machine gun was hooked to a metallic silver belt that ran around to his backpack.

This meant the team of four had just gained a very excellent, powerful machine gunner. Their chances of surviving until two o'clock instantly got even higher.

And there was also a grenade launcher thrown in with the deal, which was even better!

Ahhh, I'm so glad, Llenn thought, right at the moment that Shinohara blew up.

"Huh?"

The explosion blew Shinohara forward. The grenade had blown up right behind him and hurtled him through the air, though she didn't see it before it blew up.

"Nwaaa!" he screamed, flying through the air as Llenn watched, and smashed into the first-floor brick wall of the house headfirst. He did not move after that.

The system must have calculated that he'd broken his neck, because—*bing*—the DEAD tag glowed bright over his body.

One member of Team ZEMAL: dead.

"......"

If Llenn was stunned by what had just happened, so were Boss and Vivi, who had witnessed the same thing.

"What just happened?" asked David, who was watching the north side and couldn't see what had unfolded.

Llenn told him honestly, "Shinohara's travel companion hit him in the back with a grenade from the mist... He's dead." There was no other way to say it.

Apparently, they were dealing with someone who had no sense of honor.

"I see...a real sicko, huh?" said David, quiet anger in his voice.

Boss said, "Whoever it is, they don't have a shred of samurai honor in their bones… If I catch even a glimpse of them, I'll shoot. Don't try to stop me!"

Nobody argued with her. They didn't even comment on the samurai bit.

It was scary that Vivi didn't have anything to say. Very scary.

She cared deeply for her teammates, so her guts had to be boiling with rage.

I'm glad I'm not in the room with her, Llenn thought but did not say aloud.

And then—*Oh…wait…,* Llenn thought but did not want to think.

Who would use a grenade launcher to shoot someone they'd been working with just moments ago in the back, and not think twice? She could imagine at least one such person.

Yes, she could.

Oh…please…no…

Her pulse rose so quickly that she was afraid the AmuSphere might shut down on her. Her heartbeat was racing.

Oh no oh no oh no oh no oh no…

No, it couldn't be.

After all, M was very clear in his instructions. "Just hide. Don't go anywhere," he'd said. He gave her tactical orders.

But…

She would totally ignore a plan if there was something that seemed more fun to do…

Yes, she would do that…

Yes, I can totally imagine it…

I mean, how many years have I been friends with her?

I know this about her.

But please—! Please let it not be true!

As if to answer the cry of Llenn's heart, a vengeful voice emerged from the mist.

"Viiiviiii! You biiiiitch! Time to answer for yeeeears of your criiiiiimes!"

"Oh no," Llenn lamented, looking to the sky.

"This is a grudge maaaatch! A hundred years in the makiiiiing! I'm going to use my plasma grenades to blow that entire house off this plaaaaaaneeeeeeeeet!"

It was Fukaziroh's voice.

To be continued...

AFTERWORD

Hello, everyone, this is Keiichi Sigsawa. I'm very grateful that you've picked up *Gun Gale Online* XI.

I'm currently making the same pose that Llenn does on the cover of Volume X, with the same pistol.

No, there is no photo of this.

I'm sure you're wondering what in the world I'm talking about. I'm actually being serious for once.

The gun is an airsoft gun, however.

I'm sure you've heard about it already! (Editor's note: This is not as likely as he thinks.)

That's right, the pink pistol Llenn shoots in the story is now being sold as an air gun (technically, a "gas blowback gun")!

Tokyo Marui, one of the premier air gun makers of Japan, put out an AM.45 Version Llenn Vorpal Bunny (henceforth "Vorpal Bunny") in April of last year (2020) as an official collaboration product! I just missed out on getting to introduce it in Volume X, which came out in March!

You may recall that in the afterword of Volume IX, I introduced the pink electric air gun P90 Version Llenn and expressed my great gratitude for its existence.

This time, it's a pistol! I had already introduced the Vorpal Bunny in my story as an AM.45, a black pistol designed by Kouji Akimoto for Tokyo Marui as an original concept, and now it gets to be sold as a real air gun… As the author, I feel like I've died and gone to Heaven. My feet aren't touching the ground. It's so far below me. Uh-oh, the oxygen's getting thin up here. For being midday, the stars sure are beautiful…

On top of that, this March (2021) they started selling a plain black AM.45, the one that Pitohui uses in the story.

On the package for the Vorpal Bunny and AM.45 air guns, there are illustrations from the one and only Kouhaku Kuroboshi. The AM.45 has a brand-new illustration of Pitohui! I also wrote a special little piece for it. That's a little story you can only read there.

Its specifications as an air gun are top-notch, and its utterly original design looks awesome, of course, but on top of that, it's an ultra-rare pink handgun—so you can look good shooting it, displaying it, or doing anything with it, really.

This one is not a totally limited production like the P90, but will be manufactured and restocked at regular intervals. I'm sure it will eventually be found at reasonable prices in stores. If you find any, why not get one or two to keep on you? You can feel like Llenn or Pitohui and pretend to be a cool guy like Sigsawa!

Anyway, this has been your afterword, in the form of air gun advertisements!

I was trying to turn this afterword in as is, but my editor scolded me with a much more socially acceptable version of saying, "Cut the crap," so I'll write a little bit more.

Of course, I won't be revealing any details from the story here.

Instead, I'll give you a bit of trivia. In Japan, we use the word *netabare* to refer to advance details of a story, but I've recently learned about the English word *spoiler.* They use that word because it spoils the fun of the story.

Remember that word, because it might show up on a test. Or it might not.

It's Volume XI, everyone!

To reveal a bit of behind-the-scenes information that only the author himself and a select few knew about, *GGO* was originally designed to end at Volume IX.

But because the fans kept up with us so diligently (i.e., kept buying the books), I ended up having to write a new Squad Jam. Excuse me: I *got* to write a new Squad Jam.

It's so much fun writing *GGO* that when I was told I could keep writing it, of *course* I was going to jump at the opportunity. In other words, Volume XI was brought about by your enthusiasm, dear readers. Thank you so much.

So we've started another Squad Jam, the fifth of its kind.

If you're always working under the same rules, it's not as much fun for the players or writer or readers, so I threw in a bunch of changes right in the middle of the story, just to make the players furious.

The special rules I've written before are modeled directly off fun rules I've experienced myself in survival games (i.e., pretend battles with airsoft guns), but in this case, I decided to go one step further and make some rules that can't be done in real life.

Long live VR games, huh? The idea of getting to experience crazy gun battles in peace and safety with no one getting hurt is just the best.

If they ever make full-dive VR games, I really, really, *really* want to play *GGO*. For my weapon, I'd use the SIG SG 550.

Meanwhile, I just live my life and assume that world is coming someday. Will they make them by the time I'm an old man? Then I'll just be able to dive all day long.

The neighbors will say, "Is the old man from that house all right? I barely see him at all anymore." But I'll be fine. I'll be better than fine. I'll be *great.*

Of course, if the last two years have taught me anything, it's that you never know what will happen in the future.

But if things can turn out worse than expected, surely they can also turn out better than expected sometimes. I believe it. Sigsawa will always believe it.

With all that said, I'd like to strive for the next wave of the future, but for now, I know I need to write what comes next after this book. So once I send this file to my editor, I'll get started on that.

In the next volume, Llenn and Fukaziroh are gonna kick ass. Like always, I suppose. Look forward to that.

See you in *GGO* Volume XII.

Keiichi Sigsawa—2021

Gun grips are very
comfortable to hold,
so if they stuck
them on frying pans
like this
wouldn't that be
a really wonderful
thing to have?
Kouhaku Kuroboshi